Lisa had never known there could be such pleasure in the world. And it wasn't only physical.

Pensively, she studied the man in bed with her. He lay amid rumpled covers, with one arm thrown across his forehead.

Suppose she did have Ryder's baby. Was it fair that he would never know his child? Or that the child would never have a father?

What if the baby resembled him so strongly that, every day for the next twenty years, Lisa found herself staring into searching brown eyes, a reminder of her deception and of this brief happiness? What if she spent the rest of her life wishing she'd never left Ryder?

Maybe she shouldn't leave him.

Lisa caught her breath, scarcely daring to believe what she was considering....

SUPER ROMANCE

ABOUT THE AUTHOR

Jacqueline Diamond spent a year after college traveling and writing in Europe, an experience she drew upon for her heroine's background. Since then, she's been a news reporter, a TV columnist, the author of more than twenty Harlequin romances, and above all, a wife and mother.

Books by Jacqueline Diamond

HARLEQUIN AMERICAN ROMANCE

HARLEQUIN INTRIGUE

Let's Make a Baby!

JACQUELINE DIAMOND

HARLEQUIN®

TORONTO • NEW YORK • LONDON
AMSTERDAM • PARIS • SYDNEY • HAMBURG
STOCKHOLM • ATHENS • TOKYO • MILAN • MADRID
PRAGUE • WARSAW • BUDAPEST • AUCKLAND

ISBN 0-373-16763-6

LET'S MAKE A BABY!

Copyright © 1999 by Jackie Hyman.

This edition published by arrangement with Harlequin Books S.A.

® and TM are trademarks of the publisher. Trademarks indicated with
® are registered in the United States Patent and Trademark Office, the
Canadian Trade Marks Office and in other countries.

Printed in U.S.A.

Chapter One

"What do you mean, you want me to have a baby?"

Annalisa Maria von Schmidt De La Pena, better known as Lisa, struggled not to glare at her parents.

Glaring never worked. In fact, her tendency to thrust out her chin, set her jaw stubbornly and narrow her green eyes was almost guaranteed to land her in trouble.

So far, it had gotten her yanked from working at her father's office in Amsterdam, prevented from visiting her best friend in Rome and stuck away in a moldy old château in France's beautiful but remote Loire Valley.

"What higher aim could a daughter have than to present us with an heir?" demanded her father from halfway across the tapestried receiving room, which was the size of a soccer field and equally as cozy.

Lisa's temper got the better of her. "So now it's not a baby, it's an heir!" She gripped the arms of her straight-backed antique seat, which bore an intimidating resemblance to an electric chair. "You make me feel like some kind of broodmare!"

Before her father could respond, her mother spoke

in the quiet but authoritative manner that could make an entire ballroom full of guests fall silent.

"You are twenty-six." Although they usually conversed in Spanish or Dutch, this time Valeria von Schmidt De La Pena addressed her daughter in English, the language of business. "It is time that you married and produced a child. Not only for the sake of the company that your father has built, but for my family, too. Do not forget that we are descended from nobility."

"I haven't forgotten!" Impatiently, Lisa brushed back a strand of her long, dark hair. "But what's the rush? I want to work with Papa some more, either in Amsterdam or one of our other offices. I think I have a lot to contribute, if you'd just give me a chance!"

Her father, Schuyler, a balding man who stood a head shorter than his wife, tapped his fingers on a bowlegged end table inlaid with ivory. His determined expression reflected the formidable will that had enabled him to claw his way up from working on the docks in Amsterdam to founding a business empire.

"You are not tough enough to fill my shoes at Components International," he commented acidly. "You need to marry a strong man, one who can father offspring who have what the Americans call grit. Someday I'll need to hand over the reins, and I want it to be to my own flesh and blood. Your children!"

Lisa could feel herself bristling. Not tough enough to take over his business? Not experienced enough, certainly, but that wasn't by her own choice.

However, there was no point in pursuing the argument, when her father's glower made it clear she had no chance of winning. She decided that at least she might be able to turn this situation to her advantage.

"I'm not sure I want gritty children, but I suppose it is time I got back into circulation." And, she added silently, out of this damp château in which her parents took such pride. "Mother and I could move to the apartment in Paris."

"You have met all our eligible acquaintances in Paris," Valeria responded coolly. "And rejected them."

That was true. "As you know, my friend Nicola has invited me to visit her in Rome," Lisa reminded them. "You keep saying you'll consider it."

"Nicola no longer moves in the best circles," Schuyler said. "I realize she had good reason to divorce the baron. I do not approve of wife beaters, and you were right to stand by her. But she is in no position to sponsor you."

"Sponsor me?" Despite her best intentions, Lisa couldn't resist quirking an eyebrow. "Well, if not her, how about Maureen Buchanan? You know, the Canadian I met skiing in St. Moritz, the one who came for Christmas last year. She's dating a film director. They live in Geneva and they know lots of…"

The words trailed off. Her parents didn't even need to say anything; their frowns said it all.

Living with a man who wasn't one's husband might be tolerated in today's world. However, Maureen herself was a free spirit with neither money nor family connections who came from a Canadian city with the peculiar name of Moose Jaw.

"It isn't as if we haven't tried," her mother went on. "You've been to so many balls and dinner parties.

You could easily have chosen someone suitable, but…well, perhaps we've spoiled you.''

Lisa couldn't deny that her family had taken pains to introduce her to young men. They'd mostly been suave and attractive and, to a man, impeccably dressed.

They'd also been fixated on money and social status. Lisa had always hoped to meet someone more down to earth, a man who…

Who what? She certainly didn't want an ugly, ill-mannered slob. So what *did* she want?

She snapped back to the present as a meaningful glance passed between her parents. Too meaningful. Like a cold splash of water, the truth hit her.

They weren't talking about marriage in the abstract. They had someone in mind! An arranged marriage, like something from the Middle Ages.

Lisa supposed that, in this liberated age, she could simply refuse and, if her parents insisted, cut her ties to them. But she was their only child, and she knew how much they loved her. Needed her. Depended on her for their happiness.

Her anger faded as she noted the anxiety furrowing her mother's forehead. It was an expression Valeria had worn often since her daughter's last birthday.

She might be pampered and sheltered, but Lisa was also fiercely loyal to her family and friends. So she might as well hear them out.

''Who is he?'' she demanded.

''He?'' inquired her mother.

''This guy you want me to marry,'' she said.

Schuyler shot her a glance of respect mingled with exasperation. ''You do have a gift for reading peo-ple's minds. It gave you an edge in our marketing department—until, of course, you became so stubborn about sticking to your own ideas.''

Or rather, Lisa amended silently, until she began to develop some self-confidence and professionalism. That, she felt certain, was why her father had really sent her home from Amsterdam last year.

But this wasn't the time to refight that old battle. ''What's his name?''

''Boris Grissofsky,'' her father said gruffly. ''He owns an import-export business in Bulgaria. Also, he is descended from Austro-Hungarian nobility. His pedigree is impeccable.''

Like a stallion on a stud farm? Aloud, Lisa said, ''How well do you know him?''

''We've done several successful deals together.'' Her father's company provided parts for repairing old cars, farm equipment, airplanes and computers that, although obsolete in the West, were heavily used in other regions of the world. ''He has a keen financial sense and he can be ruthless if necessary.''

''Ruthless?'' Lisa repeated. ''Papa, we're talking about marriage, not hiring a bodyguard.''

''I know what qualities it takes to get ahead in this world!'' Her father's temper flared. ''My heir will need all of them!''

''His family is distantly related to the Hohnersteins, who as you know are an ancient noble family.'' Valeria fixed her daughter with a dark, steady gaze.

Lisa was getting a bad feeling about this, but she didn't want to reject her parents' choice out of hand. ''You wouldn't happen to have a photo?''

''Better than that,'' said her father. ''A video.''

It was, Lisa learned, already loaded into the nearest

VCR. Grimly, she moved to a couch for a better view as her father brought the TV to life.

The tape flickered, then cleared. The image was crisp and high quality; apparently Mr. Boris Grissofsky had hired a professional to film his introduction to his future wife.

On the deck of a yacht, a tuxedo-clad man struck a pose in profile. Then he swung toward the camera and extended a glass of champagne as if inviting her on board.

Lisa could forgive the hokeyness of the pose, but two other unattractive elements caught her attention. The first was Boris's nose, flattened like a boxer's. The second was a pugnaciously thick neck that looked out of place with the starched collar and white bow tie.

Still, she couldn't hold minor physical defects against him. After all, Nicola's baron had a perfect nose and an elegant neck, and he'd turned out to be a jerk.

Next, the video cut to a sidewalk café, a charming scene with flower boxes marking the edges of the dining area. Menu in hand, Boris bowed toward the camera, once again inviting her to join him.

As he straightened, a painful glint of sunlight hit his eyes and he scowled at the cameraman. For a second, his eyes revealed a naked cruelty that made Lisa shiver.

Immediately the video cut to a different angle. Once again Boris beamed affably. But she felt as if she'd seen something ugly deep within his soul.

The tape went on, showing Boris exiting a limousine and boarding a private jet. Lisa sneaked glances at her parents, but she could tell they hadn't noticed anything amiss.

Nevertheless, she trusted her instincts. As her father had said, sometimes she could almost read people's minds. In this case, what she had read in Boris's expression could fill a horror novel.

What was she going to do? She didn't even want to meet this man, let alone spend the rest of her life with him.

Tears pricked Lisa's eyes. She loved her parents. To please them, she'd suppressed the impulse to insist upon taking a role in Components International or to strike out on her own. She'd even allowed them to dictate where and how she lived.

She could see now that, without realizing it, she'd been avoiding open conflict ever since she came of age. But she couldn't marry this man.

Clearly, her parents had made up their minds. If she refused them directly, the result would be a pitched battle, the first of her life.

Nicola had disobeyed her own parents when she left the baron, and they hadn't spoken to her since. Was Lisa prepared to risk that?

The tape ended. "Well?" harrumphed her father.

"I'll think about it," she said, and fled to her room.

THE TELEPHONE was too dangerous; her mother sometimes listened on the extension. But Valeria hadn't mastered the Internet.

Lisa logged on and composed an urgent e-mail to Nicola and Maureen. They were the only people she trusted.

Nicola's other acquaintances had dropped her cold during her scandalous divorce two years earlier. Although they still socialized with Lisa, she saw them for what they were: fair-weather friends.

She sent the message and sat back in her desk chair to wait.

Afternoon sunshine washed through the many-paned windows that punctuated the length of her chamber. A canopied bed, armoire and oak wardrobe filled the far corner; a massive fireplace and several couches occupied another quarter of the room.

Closer to her, love seats were grouped around an elaborate entertainment center. This corner, nearest the door, held Lisa's computer desk, fax, color copier and overflowing bookshelves.

While she enjoyed having so much space, Lisa would have traded this château gladly for the tall, narrow house in Amsterdam where they'd lived during her childhood. The rooms had been alive with clatter from the street in front, with light that refracted off the canal in back, and with color from the tulips that crowded her window box and filled her vases.

Here, hardly any sounds penetrated, and while the walls might be covered with plaster, she could feel the cold stone beneath them. The busy world seemed far away.

Perhaps that wasn't quite fair, Lisa told herself. Through the window, she could see the April sun glimmering across green vineyards and a serenely flowing river. In the distance lay the nearest town, where dark-timbered houses surrounded an open market.

Lisa imagined she could smell the crusty bread from the village bakery. She enjoyed taking walks there, buying fruit tarts from the pastry shop and listening to the friendly chatter of housewives and store-keepers.

For a few months, she had volunteered at the local hospital, assisting the nurses and delivering flowers. But her parents had objected that people were watching her, speculating and gossiping. Under pressure from Valeria and Schuyler, Lisa had reluctantly withdrawn.

She supposed other people were sometimes curious about her. With its white spires and peaked roofs, the château resembled a storybook castle, and perhaps some townspeople cast her in the role of princess.

Unfortunately, this fairy tale had an ogre, and his name was Boris Grissofsky.

On the screen, a message popped up from Nicola. "What is so urgent?"

The Internet had become the divorcée's substitute for the social whirl she used to enjoy. Thank goodness she was at her terminal now.

Lisa typed in her story. Nicola's response came at once: "You cannot marry this man!"

"Do you know him?" As she wrote, she pictured her friend's face. A former model, Nicola had high cheekbones and wide-set eyes, with a rich mane of chestnut hair touched, at thirty-three, with the first hint of frost.

"No," Nicola wrote back. "But if you have such a bad feeling, you should listen to your heart. I wish I had heeded my intuition about the baron!"

"But how can I get out of this without antagonizing my family?"

There was a pause, and then Nicola typed, "Have a baby."

"By myself?"

"Why not? Your father wants an heir. Also, if you were already pregnant, surely this Boris would not marry you."

Lisa nibbled her lower lip. It was an interesting idea, but scary. Very scary.

She certainly did want to have children. In fact, the last time she went into town, Lisa had found herself fussing over every baby carriage that passed and watching every chubby-cheeked toddler in fascination.

Her biological clock must be nearing high noon. But it would never have occurred to her to have a child outside of marriage.

Other women did it. Took lovers, set up their own households, had babies. But not Lisa. She believed that, if possible, children deserved to have fathers as well as mothers. She was also still a virgin.

Over the years, there'd been more than one opportunity to lose her virginity. None of the men had touched her heart, however. Then there was the danger of discovery by the tabloid press.

She shuddered at the prospect of seeing her disgrace splattered across newsstands. "Heiress in love nest!" or, worse, "Secret photos! Heiress bares all for love!" The notion was enough to drive desire completely from her mind.

Still, circumstances had changed. Her parents wanted an heir; they'd emphasized that more than the need of a husband for her. Maybe Nicola was right.

"How could I arrange to have a baby?" Lisa typed back.

"Clinic," came the terse response.

A baby from a frozen vial? She grimaced. It sounded so...cold.

Besides, how could she be sure the man had the right qualities to appease her father? Above all, she could never be sure some clinic employee might not yield to the temptation to sell the information to the press.

"I don't think so," she wrote back. "But thanks for the suggestion."

They chatted a while longer before signing off. Lisa was about to change for dinner when a message from Maureen slashed across the screen.

"Well? Tell all!"

She repeated her story. This time it was Maureen's face, freckled and alert, that filled her mind. She could visualize the intrigued expression as her friend listened and the habit of pushing a wedge of reddish hair behind one ear.

"That video of Boris Grissofsky was for you?" Maureen tapped. "He hired Win—" that was her filmmaker boyfriend "—to shoot it! He paid well, too. The first check bounced, but he made good."

Win took video jobs to support himself between making low-budget films. He always seemed in need of financing. The one time Lisa had met him, he'd hinted that her family might invest in his next feature, but Maureen had silenced him.

"What's Boris like?" she wrote back. "Have you met him?"

"Not me," typed Maureen. "Win says he's cranky. You aren't going to marry him, are you?"

Lisa repeated Nicola's suggestion about having a baby by herself, along with her reservation about using a clinic.

"Forget the test tubes!" Maureen wrote back promptly. "Pick a guy and do it the fun way!"

Lisa groaned aloud. "Oh, sure."

"How hard can it be?" wrote her friend. "Get an ovulation kit, make sure the timing's right and go somewhere in disguise."

"Make love to a stranger?" Lisa made a face at her computer screen. "That's dangerous."

"You worry too much." Maureen herself was fearless, having left home right after high school, worked at numerous jobs and traveled extensively. "Besides, it wouldn't have to be a total stranger. We could check him out."

Maureen had a ready answer for Lisa's next objection, too. The risk of being recognized? She should go to America, where the De La Penas were virtually unknown. Win had a lot of contacts, one of whom could get her a fake passport, so she wouldn't even have to use her own name.

The need to find a nobleman? "Forget that! You've got enough blue blood yourself. As for grit, Americans are famous for it!"

"Thanks," Lisa wrote. "But I don't think so."

"I'll make inquiries," responded her friend. "Be on-line tomorrow morning at nine." She signed off before Lisa could protest.

Lisa had begun to hope that her parents wouldn't press too hard, but she found out differently at dinner. Her father mentioned introducing her to Boris and scowled when Lisa said she needed more time to think about it. Had a meeting already been arranged? she wondered.

She didn't sleep well that night. On awakening, she recalled a long, troubled dream in which she fled from a many-headed monster, only to find every door closed to her.

Hot coffee and a croissant eased her anxiety a little. By 9:00 a.m. she was back on-line, surprised to discover that she no longer felt quite so dismayed at the notion of having a baby by herself.

Well, not exactly by herself.

She didn't like the idea of losing her virginity to a man who wasn't her husband. But could that be any worse than losing it to—shudder—Boris?

Maureen's message popped on the screen at 9:10. "You there? Still holding firm against your parents?"

"Bloody but unbowed."

"Here's the scoop." Maureen chattered away when she typed, just as she did in person. "I asked Win for his opinion..."

"You didn't tell him about the baby!"

"Of course not! Well, I told him I knew *someone* who wanted to have a baby, but I didn't mention your name."

"Wouldn't it be obvious?"

"Men don't pay attention to things like that," her friend wrote. "Anyway, I said you want to keep it anonymous and that you'd like to find an American father. He came up with a terrific idea!"

"What is it?" Lisa asked warily.

"A matchmaker!" wrote Maureen. "Well, not exactly a matchmaker. A detective."

While making a public-relations video for a company in California the previous year, she said, Win had met a private investigator who was gathering background on a fugitive embezzler. The man specialized in finding missing persons.

"You think I should hire him to find a daddy?" Lisa typed.

"That's what Win suggested," replied her friend.

"He said I could look up the guy's Web Page. So I did. His name is Ryder Kelly, and guess what? He's cute!"

"Maureen, you're not proposing that I sleep with this detective?"

"Why not?" wrote her friend. "He's an ex-Marine and a former cop. How's that for tough and self-sufficient, eh? Also unmarried."

"He put that on his Web Page?"

"To show that he's ready to go wherever and whenever he's needed. One of the things he does is track down bail jumpers."

"He's a bounty hunter?" Lisa got a mental image of a cowboy in the Wild West, leaning forward in the saddle as he lassoed a varmint. "He doesn't ride around on a horse, does he?" she joked.

"See for yourself." Maureen sent her the Internet address and added, "Don't chicken out. It's time you took your life into your own hands." She signed off without waiting for a reply.

Lisa stared at the screen. She couldn't believe she was actually considering this crazy scheme.

How ironic, that getting pregnant out of wedlock, which would once have meant scandal and shame, might be more acceptable to her parents than simply rejecting Boris, moving out and getting a job. So Lisa hoped, anyway.

They'd emphasized that they wanted her to have a child who could carry on the business and the family name, right? They had no great fondness for Boris. He was simply an acceptable figure to drop into the role of her husband.

Acceptable to them, but not to her. On the other hand, what about this bounty hunter?

Lisa typed in his Web Page address, and in a moment she was staring at a colorful ad for Ryder Kelly Investigations. A photo at the top showed a man with a strong face and light brown hair cut no-nonsense short.

The information confirmed what Maureen had told her: Ryder Kelly was a private investigator specializing in missing persons. It listed references, including the head of security at a major corporation and a police captain in the LAPD who had been Ryder's supervisor.

A daddy-to-be with references, she thought. How perfect.

She clicked on the photo and suddenly the man's face turned toward her. Dark eyes searched Lisa's face, and for an instant she felt as if he were looking directly at her.

A deep, steady voice spoke from the screen. "I'm glad you found me," he said. "Now let me find whoever you're looking for."

Startled, Lisa felt as if she'd been caught sneaking around. Then she began to smile. It was a clever ad. The man had intelligence and nerve. Not to mention references.

Of course, she needed to know a few more things about him before she would feel comfortable selecting him as the father of her baby. But those were the kind of things she could only determine in person.

A baby. The idea began to take on reality. A sweet-faced infant whom she could hold in her arms and nurture and love. She wouldn't even mind the dirty diapers: at the hospital, she'd helped in the nursery, so she knew what to expect.

The strength of her longing surprised Lisa. A child

would fill her life with commitment and joy. Besides, surely her parents couldn't object to an heir who carried both the De La Pena genes and those of the intense, rough-hewn Ryder Kelly.

As she logged off, Lisa realized that she had made a decision. Whether or not she ultimately decided to let this man impregnate her, she was definitely going to America to meet him.

She would need to buy an ovulation kit and determine the best time to conceive. Then, with Maureen's help, she would embark on the greatest adventure of her life.

Chapter Two

Ryder was waiting his turn on top of the mountain when he noticed the woman below, near the ski lodge.

First, a glint of sunlight off her binoculars caught his eye. Long black hair fell across her shoulders and, despite her ski jacket and pants, she had a sleek figure that made everyone around her seem bulky by comparison.

She lowered the binoculars, revealing an exotic, oval face, and Ryder let out a low whistle of appreciation. Although she radiated confidence, there was an innocence about her that made him want to find out how innocent she really was.

Man, you're flipping out. That lady is the last thing you need.

Adjusting his sunglasses against the snow's glare, he turned his attention to a queue of people below him and to one side, on the intermediate slope. Just about the time Ryder would be ready to launch himself down the mountain, so would Mr. Joe Ortiz, alias Joseph Orton.

He'd had the man under surveillance since early yesterday. Ortiz had proved an elusive target, but his own greed was guiding him into Ryder's hands.

Right in front of Ortiz stood his latest target, a sixtyish woman with expensive ski gear. Ryder didn't know her particulars, but he was sure "Joe the O" had already checked out her bank account and was well on his way to taking possession of it.

Down near the lodge, a young man in a fisherman sweater approached the young black-haired woman. She flashed him a smile that lit up the afternoon shadows, but politely shook her head.

The man retreated reluctantly. Miss Innocence swung her binoculars into place and, for one startled moment, Ryder could have sworn she was staring directly at him.

She glanced quickly away. Too quickly. She *had* been staring at him.

Before he could control it, speculation shimmered across Ryder's mental landscape. Exactly how far did her interest extend? How would she look without that jacket, or anything else, just a waterfall of dark hair spilling over her personal landmarks?

He caught himself abruptly. First of all, judging by her designer ski clothes, the lady had bucks. Not only that, but she held herself too regally for his taste.

Ryder didn't like spoiled princesses. And if the lady turned out not to be a snob, he knew from experience she was likely to be in search of Mr. Right. That was the modern trend: commitment.

Not for him. Ryder needed movement in his life—excitement, danger, fresh challenges. He could never be anyone's pet poodle, and he was too honest to mislead women. Which meant he'd been spending a lot of nights alone.

He jerked his attention back to his surroundings as the skier directly ahead of him pushed off. Below, it was Mrs. Target's turn, but she was fussing over one of her boots and holding up the line.

If Ryder went now, he'd be too early. Time for a show of chivalry to the skier behind him, except that, when he turned, he found himself facing not a woman but a hulking guy with tattoos decorating his neck.

Ryder caught a mouthful of cold air and coughed. That gave him an excuse. "Something in my throat," he sputtered. "You go ahead."

"Thanks, pal." The bruiser started past, then paused to whack Ryder on the back. "Hope that helps!" Away he skied.

Now Ryder was coughing in earnest. Below, Joe the O's intended victim had finally wobbled her way onto the slope, and the fugitive himself was taking off in her wake.

That left no time to gauge an exact route. Ryder prepared for a whirlwind descent and hoped his haste wouldn't make an already tricky plan downright impossible.

After a bondsman posted $100,000 bail, Joe the O had skipped out of California pending trial on charges that he romanced a widow out of her insurance money. Bail had been set high because it was his third offense, and he faced a twenty-five-years-to-life sentence.

Joe was notoriously suspicious of anyone trying to befriend him, so Ryder intended to try the dangerous maneuver of a near collision on the ski slope. Since Joe had only recently taken up the sport, it should be easy to panic him into falling.

Ryder would insist on driving him to a doctor's office. Or, if that tactic failed, he would hint that he was so fearful of a lawsuit that he might be arm-twisted into paying Joe off, if they could just go somewhere alone to discuss it.

Joe never could pass up an easy mark.

Body low, muscles pumping, Ryder zoomed across the brilliant white surface, jetting around the moguls and past signs warning advanced skiers to stay off the intermediate slope. It was a good thing, Ryder reflected as he swung toward Joe, that he loved breaking the rules.

His main concern, as he spotted Joe teetering and flailing his way down the hill, was that his quarry would collapse on his own. Then, with a jolt of alarm, Ryder saw that the fugitive was heading in the wrong direction. Very wrong.

Oblivious to everything but his own fear of falling, Joe was staggering off the intermediate slope onto the one marked for beginners. Granted, that was where he actually belonged, but the space was already occupied by a group of youngsters practicing snowplow stops.

Ryder had a hunch Joe hadn't mastered that particular move yet. Otherwise he wouldn't be careening toward a group of kids who were only now glancing up, registering alarm and struggling to move out of his way.

Suddenly Ryder's little game of waylaying Joe took on real urgency. The inexperienced man might not be traveling very fast, but he was a lot bigger than those kids. A collision could result in snapped bones or worse.

Ryder pushed with his poles and crouched low to pick up speed. Tension gripped his thigh muscles, his back, his forearms. He had to catch up with Joe in time to knock him away from those youngsters.

It wasn't going to be easy. Quite a distance separated them, and it was obstructed by other skiers, moguls and a discarded pole.

Ryder veered around one impediment after another and took a shortcut that sent him shooting off a rocky drop. He flew for several seconds before hitting the snow with jarring impact.

Ahead Joe was closing fast on the fleeing children. One little girl stumbled and toppled. She lay in a jumble of blond hair and brightly striped clothing, directly in Joe's path.

The pudgy con man stabbed at the snow with his poles, trying to stop himself. It apparently never occurred to him, however, that he might deliberately take a fall in order to spare someone else. In another few yards he would run right over the little girl.

There was no time to maneuver. Coming at Joe from above, Ryder slammed directly into him with a churning, crunching thud that knocked the air out of his own lungs. The impact flung them both off their feet and scattered their poles and skis across the snow.

Ryder felt himself whirling into a void as he slid across the snow and landed in a heap. He refused to yield to his dizziness, to allow himself to black out.

Never lose control. Never give in.

After a moment the earth stopped spinning and he became aware of people shouting. Snow fanning into the air as other skiers arrived. A child crying.

With an effort he lifted his head. Light dazzled his eyes; he must have lost his sunglasses in the collision. It took a moment before his pupils adjusted enough to survey the scene.

To one side, the little girl struggled to her feet,

unharmed. A short distance below, Joe lay with one leg crooked at an unnatural angle.

There was nothing wrong with his lungs, though. Ryder could tell from the way the man's curses were turning the air blue.

He became aware of a sharp pain in his right ankle. It didn't look as if he were in any shape to offer Joe a ride to the hospital. On the other hand, the lawsuit angle might work really well.

Something blotted the light. Ryder blinked and wondered if he were passing out after all.

Then he inhaled a delicate, tantalizing scent he couldn't identify. If pushed, he would have described it as the essence of springtime, which was odd, because he was not normally given to metaphors.

Thick black hair curtained his face, and he found himself gazing into the greenest eyes he'd ever seen. And a face Botticelli would have killed to paint. It was, he realized with dazed admiration, the woman with the binoculars.

"Are you all right?" asked a lightly accented voice.

It should have been a simple question to answer, but Ryder had a hard time sorting out his tongue from the rest of his mouth. "Uh" was what came out.

The woman stroked his wrist—at least, it seemed to be his—and placed her fingers on his pulse. "It feels steady."

"Really?" That surprised him. He could have sworn his heart was beating out a staccato rhythm worthy of some Caribbean steel drum band. "Are you a nurse?"

Confusion fleeted across her face. "Well...yes, sort

of." She gulped. "I need to ask you a few medical questions."

"Go ahead." He would tell her almost anything if it would keep her nearby. Who needed a normal pulse rate, anyway?

"When did you have your last complete physical?" She studied him intently, as if his answer mattered to her in some personal way.

"Last month."

"Blood work, too?"

"Of course." He groaned as pain spiked through his ankle. "My business...insurance requires it."

"How are your personal habits?" Long, dark lashes screened her gaze, and he could have sworn her cheeks were turning pink. "Sexually speaking."

"Monastic. What's that got to do with my ankle?"

"You hurt your ankle?"

This was the oddest medical exam he'd ever had. "That's right, Nurse." Ryder would have said more, but his peripheral vision caught a flash of movement. He turned to see two men carting Joe the O away on a stretcher. "I have to catch up with him. Could you help me..."

Out of nowhere loomed a young fellow in a white ski jacket. "I'm Dr. Witt, the house physician. Are you hurt?"

"It's his ankle," the black-haired woman explained, and moved back to give the doctor room. To Ryder's relief, she showed no sign of leaving.

He wasn't sure why he was so anxious for her to stay. Just curiosity, he supposed. And the fact that his blood was singing a ballad of masculine desire.

Of course, he knew better than to follow through

on it. This lady was too fresh, too sexy, too well dressed, too *everything*.

Below, the attendants were loading Joe into an ambulance. Ryder gestured toward them. "Where are they taking him?"

"To the hospital, where they're going to take you next," said the doctor.

Fighting to hold back a groan, Ryder sat up. He half expected the others to react to the scream of his muscles and the loud throbbing of his bruises, but no one seemed to hear them except the black-haired woman, who winced in empathy. "I might have sprained my ankle but I don't need to be hospitalized."

"Right or left?"

"Right." As the fellow checked his leg, Ryder took out his cellular phone and rapid-dialed the bail bondsman. To the doctor, he said, "What's the name of the hospital?"

"Saint Something-or-other. It's the only one in town." The man shrugged apologetically. "I just got here last week."

"Can I help with something?" asked the green-eyed lady, hovering over him like a guardian angel.

"Just stay there," Ryder said as he listened to the phone ring. "You inspire me."

She smiled. At the sight, his rigidly held libido flamed into a state of fevered longing. His body stopped hurting and started composing poetry.

"Yeah, hello? Speak up!" snarled the bail bondsman into his ear.

Tersely Ryder told him where he could find his missing client.

"Bring him in yourself," snapped the man.

"I got injured." Ryder knew Mr. O was due for arraignment in two days. If he weren't brought in by then, the bail would be forfeited to the court. "No way I can get him there on time. I'm telling you right where he is, flat on his back. You want him or not?"

The man thought it over for about a dollar's worth of phone time. Then he said, "Yeah, okay."

"You know where to send the check." Ryder had dealt with the man before.

"Yeah." With no further ado, the bail bondsman hung up.

"It doesn't seem to be broken," said the doctor. "But I'd recommend an X ray, to make sure."

Ryder hated hospitals. Lying around being poked and scanned was not his idea of a productive activity. "Just wrap it, will you?"

"I'm happy to do that, but I don't see how I can discharge you yet," the doctor said. "You incurred quite a jolt. Any dizziness? Nausea?"

"Only at the thought of hospital food."

The doctor's forehead puckered. "You seem alert, but there could be some undetected brain injury. The swelling sometimes doesn't show up until later."

"I can take care of him," volunteered the guardian angel, who didn't seem to notice that half the males on the slope were staring at her. In fact, if she didn't depart soon, Ryder figured the accident rate around here was going to start soaring. "If he gets sick, I could take him to the emergency room."

The doctor gestured to a resort employee, who hurried to help support Ryder. "Then I guess we can take care of your husband in my clinic, ma'am. We'll just need for him to sign a waiver."

"Fine," Ryder said.

The woman kept close behind as they descended. He was glad she hadn't denied being his wife, under the circumstances.

But why *was* she being so friendly? Maybe she thought she knew him from somewhere. But Ryder had never seen her before. He would have remembered.

Could she be some kind of female con artist who'd mistaken him for a millionaire ski buff? Not in these worn jeans and patched jacket. The Army Surplus ski boots weren't particularly impressive, either.

Maybe she was a Good Samaritan. If not, he would figure out her game soon enough.

A short time later, his ankle bandaged and a pair of lightweight crutches tucked under his arms, Ryder was a free man. In no shape to drive, though.

"I'll give you a lift." The woman accompanied him out of the building, moving with such grace that he felt like a robot clunking along beside her. "After all, you saved that little girl. You're a hero."

Once upon a time, that description might have thrilled Ryder Kelly, the kid from a trailer park who'd set out to conquer the world. Now it just made him wary.

He wasn't anybody's hero. But he did need a ride. Not to mention the kind of loving care this lady seemed willing to give.

He knew he was being foolish. This looked like a setup if he'd ever seen one. Or else an invitation to a dance from which he would have to excuse himself early.

But Ryder was willing to let this vision play her little game a while longer. For one thing, he was still light-headed from the painkiller the doctor had given him. Besides, he had a feeling that, one way or another, he was likely to come out on top.

BORIS GRISSOFSKY'S pager went off during a most inconvenient moment in the apartment of his mistress. It was several minutes before he could excuse himself to go outside, on the pretext of having a smoke, and return the call from his cellular phone.

He lit up, inhaled deeply and dialed the number of his personal assistant.

"Lothaire Warner here."

"It's me. What do you want?" Boris frowned as people brushed past him in the square, sometimes breaking stride as they caught sight of his phone. Sofia, Bulgaria, was still recovering from its Communist austerity, and high-tech appendages were not yet taken for granted.

"I have received word from Miss De La Pena's maid that she has left the château and caught a flight to New York." The young assistant had accompanied Boris on his recent visit to the De La Penas, and had secured a spy within the inner sanctum.

"New York?" During the visit, Annalisa had barely spoken to Boris, but her parents had been most talkative. No one had mentioned planning any trips, however. "For what purpose?"

"According to the maid, she left a note saying that she was going to see a friend and would return on Tuesday."

"Does the maid know of any friends in America?"

"No."

Boris gritted his teeth, which had the effect of chomping his Turkish cigarette in half. Coughing and choking, he spat the harsh tobacco into the road, narrowly missing a girl on a motor scooter.

This was disturbing news. The ice princess had made it clear she didn't like Boris. He didn't much like her, either. But he liked her money, and her reputation for obedience.

She would marry him. She must marry him. He owed a fortune to a group of Russian gangsters, and they were not known for their patience.

This trip to America might indicate rebellion on Annalisa's part, but perhaps it was only a childish escapade meant to annoy her parents. He must not panic. "Find out where she goes after she lands."

"Naturally," said his assistant. Lothaire had a way with computers and had already scoped out the family's credit card numbers, so she shouldn't be difficult to track.

Boris hoped, for all their sakes, that the pretty heiress would jet home again like a good girl. If not, he would do whatever he must to bring her in line.

Once they were married there would be no more such stunts. What Boris owned, he controlled absolutely.

Whether she liked it or not, Miss De La Pena was going to join his list of possessions.

LISA COULDN'T BELIEVE she'd actually gotten Ryder Kelly into her rental car. She supposed he must be wondering at her sudden interest, but didn't men and women meet this way—well, more or less—all the time?

It was beyond Lisa's experience, of course. Like practically everything that had happened in the past month.

She'd been correct in guessing that a meeting with Boris had already been scheduled. Little more than a week after she learned of his existence, he'd shown up at the château, full of shallow flattery and hints about his vast wealth.

She didn't like the possessive way he stared at her. She didn't like the way, when he held her hand, he was always twiddling his fingers and rubbing his thumb back and forth. Everything about him made her skin crawl.

To her dismay, there had been talk of a wedding. Perhaps at Christmas, her mother had said. Why not early fall, while the weather was fine? Boris had countered. The sooner the better.

After he left, Lisa had tried to persuade her parents that he was unsuitable. Her mother's back had gone stiff and she'd averted her gaze. Schuyler had shouted angrily that she was "selfish" and "ungrateful."

Every night she'd gone to bed with her heart aching and tears pricking her eyes. The only consolation had been the ovulation kit she picked up in the village and the supportive e-mails from Maureen and Nicola.

A week ago the fake passport came in the mail from Switzerland, tucked inside a fashion magazine in case her mother opened the package. Two days ago Maureen had called Ryder's office pretending to work for a large corporation that wanted to hire him in a hurry and had talked the secretary into disclosing that he was at a ski resort in Colorado.

As she navigated the road from the ski slopes to the town below, Lisa sneaked a glance at the man beside her. He did an impressive job of filling the front seat, with his long legs and broad shoulders.

From the moment she'd spotted him on top of the

mountain, Lisa had become aware of his restless energy. He had riveted her attention even before she recognized him.

In this enclosed space, she could feel the air vibrating. It was hard to believe the man's sexual habits were really monastic, but that would explain his edginess.

Lisa wished she knew more about the subject. Her parents shielded her from risqué movies and books, and while she'd acquired a textbook knowledge of what intercourse involved, she had trouble reconciling it with the longing she sometimes felt to be held and stroked.

It scared and excited her to realize she was about to discover the facts for herself. Here sat Ryder Kelly, masculinity personified. Complete with watchful brown eyes and a hard, agile body. Also a clean bill of health, except for that injured ankle.

I'm going to make love to this man. We're going to take our clothes off and I'm going to let him touch me everywhere.

Sheer panic nearly blinded Lisa, and she slowed the car. This wouldn't do.

"Something wrong?" asked the man beside her.

"I just wondered where you're staying," she said through a clogged throat.

"Turn right at the stop sign," he said. "Go up the hill, take the second left. It's the fourth house on the right."

"Thanks."

She could drop him off, Lisa told herself. She could drive away a virgin. Intact. Safe.

Until she walked down the aisle with Boris.

Anything but that!

According to the ovulation kit, the timing was perfect. This weekend. This man. She had to do it.

What about his ankle? What if it hurt too much? Maybe she should call Maureen for instructions.

No. She had sworn to have no contact with anyone she knew, not while she was here in disguise. In today's computerized world, it would be too easy for Ryder to trace her if she did. Assuming, of course, that he ever wanted to.

"You know," murmured his baritone voice, "I'm not big on small talk. But would it be too much of a strain to tell me your name?"

"Lisa Schmidt," she said.

He waited, then added, "This is the part where you ask my name."

"I heard you tell the doctor," she said.

"So, we can move on to some other scintillating topic." Tilting his head, he regarded her with amused irony. "Let's see, you're a nurse. Where do you live?"

Lisa had prepared a story, but in that one she'd been an executive from a multinational firm, scouting ski resorts for acquisition. Not a nurse. She'd seized on Ryder's suggestion because it gave her an excuse to ask medical questions, but now she had to come up with a new scenario, fast.

"I'm from Florida." It was the first thing that popped into her mind. Crazy idea. All she knew about Florida was that they had Disney World and alligators.

"Florida in general or some city in particular?"

"Miami," she said, and instantly realized that she had mispronounced it.

"Mee-ami?" he said.

"Spain, before that," Lisa improvised. Realizing he was likely to ask for a city, she added, "Barcelona." At least she knew how to pronounce that.

"I didn't realize nurses moved around so much."

"I'm a student nurse," she said.

"Specializing in asking accident victims about their sexual habits?"

Lisa started to laugh. This conversation was rapidly turning ridiculous, and she couldn't pretend otherwise. "All right, I'm not a nurse."

"And you don't live in Mee-ami?"

"No."

"Care to tell me where you really live and what you really do?"

"No." They reached the top of the hill, and she turned left.

"You could have said you were an insurance claims adjuster for the ski resort." He quirked an eyebrow.

"Would you have believed me?"

He shook his head.

"There you have it. Ask me no questions, I'll tell you no lies."

"Oh, but I think I've earned the right to ask you one particular question." His tone was low and dark. Lisa didn't know why, but it sent electricity sparking through her nervous system.

"And what might that be?"

"What are *your* sexual habits?"

Fourth house on the right. A two-story A-frame made of split logs and scalloped Swiss-style.

Push had come to shove.

"I guess you're about to find out," said Lisa.

Chapter Three

Nothing about this woman made sense, which aroused Ryder's suspicions. Unfortunately, she also aroused him, period.

He knew only two things about Lisa Schmidt. One, she was an irresistible mixture of jumpy naîveté and barely restrained sexuality. Second, she was a lousy liar.

Not a con artist, then. More likely a young professional on holiday, letting her hair down and seeking a little fun. Ryder didn't intend to serve as casual entertainment, not even for a woman beautiful enough to make his socks stand up under their own power.

"Aren't you taking me for granted?" he inquired as the car halted in front of the chalet. "I've already told you my sexual habits are monastic."

Her green eyes widened and then her lips curved ruefully. "You're right, I *was* making an assumption. I hope you're not offended."

He swung his door open and reached into the back for his crutches. "I'm not. Nor am I available. Thanks for the ride, Lisa, and I hope you enjoy your vacation."

"You can't send me away!" The alarm in her voice stopped him.

"Why not?"

"You need me."

"I do?" he said.

"Someone will have to drive you back tomorrow to pick up your car," she said.

"I'll call a cab."

"Well, I need you."

"For what?" he said.

"Let's go inside and I'll tell you." Without waiting for a response, Lisa opened her door and came around to assist him.

Ryder didn't like to accept help, but his ankle hurt in spite of the painkiller. Besides, he was curious to hear what she would say next.

Also, he discovered as he tried to propel himself upright, his bruised muscles had become annoyingly weak. He stumbled on the metal crutches and would have fallen against the car had Lisa not caught his elbow.

Calmly and without fuss, she helped him regain his balance. Despite her skittish responses during their verbal sparring, Ryder discovered that there was something steady about Lisa Schmidt.

As she guided him up the icy walkway, she didn't pester him with silly reassurances or give him a pep talk. She just supported his arm, pointed to a half step that he hadn't noticed and guided him onto the chalet's porch.

Ryder hesitated as he put the key in the lock. There was always a risk in letting a stranger inside, especially when he was not operating at full capacity.

He'd seen enough of life to know that danger could flare when least expected.

But he'd never been afraid to take chances. He didn't intend to start now, especially when it would mean never finding out what circumstances had thrown this intriguing woman into his path.

Ryder gestured Lisa inside ahead of him. Following her, he had to maneuver carefully across the thick blue pile carpet.

It snagged his crutches. Furthermore, he was conscious of every movement for fear of knocking over an expensive vase or cut-glass dish.

The chalet belonged to Nina McNally, the widow flimflammed by Joe the O. When Ryder had questioned Nina, she'd mentioned bringing Joe here and teaching him to ski. That had reminded her of the way Joe had perked up when he noticed how many well-dressed older women frequented the slopes.

She'd speculated that Joe might return here to try to get his hands on someone else's money. Anxious for Ryder to capture her seducer, she had happily loaned him the chalet. He made a mental note to send her a bouquet of flowers as a thank-you.

"How weird." Lisa gazed with an odd expression at the blue rug, white walls with blue molding, blue-and-white furniture and blue knickknacks.

"What's wrong?" he asked as he sank into a chair.

"It's so blue," she said.

"I'm just staying here for the weekend. I didn't choose the color scheme."

"It's…unusual. No big deal." She shrugged out of her jacket. Beneath it lurked a rose-colored blouse of spun-sugar silk that clung to her curves. She was so slender that the fullness of her breasts caught Ryder off guard, and he had to force himself to look away.

"What did you need me for?" he said.

"Can I fix you something to eat?" Lisa started toward the hallway.

"Why are you changing the subject?"

"Because I'm uncomfortable with it." She stopped to examine some blue glass goblets on a mirrored shelf.

"Or because you need time to make up another story?"

She turned toward him. "I wish I could. I'm lousy at thinking on my feet."

"So tell me the truth." Ryder itched to walk over, catch her by the shoulders and demand an answer. If only he was sure he could even move. "You said you need me. Why?"

Long, dark lashes veiled her eyes. She folded her arms around herself protectively as she forced out the words. "I need to seduce you."

"Excuse me?"

Usually Ryder only noticed body language when he was trying to gain an advantage on a quarry, but now he found himself attuned to everything about Lisa. Even her nose. It was thin, with an aristocratic curve and an expressive tip that, just now, quivered as she weighed her response.

"There was another man," she said finally. "A man who turned out to be not very nice. I need someone to…help me recover. When I saw you on the slope, I decided that man was you."

"Whoa!" Alarm lifted Ryder halfway out of the chair before pain dropped him back. "You must have me confused with somebody else. I'm nobody's knight in shining armor.''

''You saved that little girl.''

''I'm great at five-minute rescues.'' Ryder wondered how she could have misjudged him so badly. ''Let's get one thing straight. I can't stand having people hang expectations on me or try to fence me in. I function best alone.''

Lisa moved to the couch and perched on its arm. He was puzzled to read relief in her gaze. ''That's what I want, too.''

''To go to bed with me and then leave?''

''I can't handle another relationship right now,'' she said. ''But this man made me feel bad about myself and men in general. I need to get past that.''

Although she spoke earnestly, there was an opaqueness in her gaze that Ryder couldn't penetrate. She might be lying again and covering it more skillfully. Or perhaps she was simply embarrassed about her proposal.

''You just picked me out with your binoculars— yes, I saw you looking—and decided to seduce me?'' Ryder asked skeptically.

''You're very attractive.'' She spoke without coyness, as if reciting an obvious fact. ''Don't women do this all the time?''

''Not in my experience,'' he said. ''I'm not saying I don't get propositioned once in a while. Usually the lady's too out of control for my taste, or she wants a bigger piece of me than I'm prepared to give.''

''I only want one piece of you,'' she said, and turned a vivid shade of scarlet.

''How flattering.''

She got even redder. "I'm sorry. That didn't come out the way I meant it."

"You honestly believe a roll in the hay is going to get this jerk out of your system?" He studied her dubiously. "How old are you?"

"Twenty-six." She lifted her chin, pride reasserting itself. "Yes, I think so, if it's the right roll in the hay, as you put it."

Why was he hesitating? Ryder wondered. His ankle hurt and the medication made him woozy, but it wouldn't take much stimulation to overcome those disadvantages.

He wanted the woman. He'd craved her from the first moment he glimpsed her.

But he didn't trust strokes of good luck. Something was fishy about this situation, and he needed to get to the bottom of it.

Outside, the afternoon shadows grew long. He felt weary down to his bones.

"I'll have to think it over," he said. "In the meantime, did I hear you offer me something to eat?"

"Sure!" With a will-o'-the-wisp smile, Lisa popped off the couch and disappeared down the hallway.

"There's not much in the fridge!" Ryder called. "You'll have to open a can of something!"

"Okay!" came the reply.

Even in her absence, her teasing scent undulated through his senses. Ryder leaned back, enjoying his awareness of this intriguing woman and trying to absorb the day's events.

He'd nailed Joe the O. If the bail bondsman acted with his usual efficiency, the man would hobble out of the hospital and go directly to jail.

It was time for Ryder to get back to Los Angeles and pick up his messages. He had some odds and ends to finish, and there were usually other assignments available, locating runaway kids and spying on unfaithful spouses.

On the other hand, putting too much stress on an injured ankle was a sure way to worsen the injury, and tomorrow was Sunday. A day of leisure would be exactly what the doctor ordered.

And Lisa? Was she what the doctor ordered, or was she trouble personified?

A tinny banging emanated from the kitchen, as if someone were hammering on metal. Before Ryder could call out a question, a *crash* sounded, accompanied by a squeal of alarm.

"Lisa? Are you all right?" He hoisted himself out of the depths of his chair and reached for his crutches.

"It's a mess!" she cried. "Don't come in here!"

How could anyone have so much trouble opening a can? As he lurched forward, Ryder supposed the lady must have been trying to whip up something fancy.

He hopped and thumped his way down the short hallway to the gleaming kitchen. Formerly gleaming. As he entered, he saw that something red spattered the entire room, from the cabinets to the tile floor.

For a horrified moment, he thought Lisa had been badly cut, but then he saw her trying to sponge off the crimson-smeared refrigerator door with ineffectual swipes. In the middle of the floor sat a smashed can of tomato soup.

On the counter lay an ice pick and a screwdriver. It took Ryder several seconds to figure out that she'd been using them to try to open the can.

A woebegone face turned toward him. Tomato soup dripped from Lisa's black hair, silk blouse and ski pants, all the way down to her designer boots.

Ryder pointed to an electrical device on the counter. "That's a can opener." He opened a drawer and pulled out a weighted tool equipped with gear wheels. "This is a can opener." He pointed to the ice pick and the screwdriver. "Neither of those is a can opener."

"I'm a little out of practice when it comes to cooking," said Lisa as a glob of tomato soup plopped from the sponge onto the floor.

"At cleaning up, too. Lady, did you just get out of an institution or are you always like this?"

"I don't usually screw up this bad," she said. "Is cooking a prerequisite?"

"To what?"

"Seducing you," she said.

Despite his best intentions, Ryder could feel himself getting hard. How could the woman radiate sensuality while covered with red goop? Maybe it was the vulnerability in her eyes, or the humor quirking at the edges of her full lips, or the way her dampened blouse clung to her full breasts.

Maybe it was something else entirely—the sense that a loopy, endearing human being had just landed in his life. Someone full of surprises and very much worth exploring.

"Forget the cooking," he said. "Let's hit the shower."

LISA KNEW she should be overjoyed. Her plan was working perfectly.

She'd nearly lost her composure when she walked

into the chalet and found it overwhelmingly blue. It reminded her of the stick in the ovulation kit, telling her that it was the optimal time to conceive.

In the face of Ryder's questions, she'd struggled desperately for a new story that she could tell convincingly. She'd stuck as close as possible to the truth and, to her amazement, it seemed to have worked.

But now that Ryder believed her and wanted her, she wasn't sure she could go through with it.

"Did you hear me?" he repeated. "I offered to take a shower with you."

Swallowing hard, Lisa grabbed a kitchen towel and dabbed at her blouse. "I think we ought to clean up in here first."

His mouth twisted knowingly. "I see."

"See what?"

"That I intimidate you."

She glanced up, startled by the truth of what he'd said. Standing upright in the enclosed space, Ryder loomed even larger than he'd appeared on the slope.

She became aware of his arrogantly tilted head, his broad shoulders and his strong arms. Of the cowboy-style flannel shirt stretched across a muscular chest, and the faded jeans that hugged his lean hips. Even more significantly, she noticed the thrust of those hips, hinting at—no, shouting of—masculine potency.

"You do intimidate me," she said. "That's why I chose you."

"Because you're afraid of me?" Light through the kitchen window gleamed across the burnished skin of his face and neck. She wondered if he were equally tanned beneath the shirt, and how those muscles would feel if she ran her hands over them.

"I'm not afraid of you," she said. "The point is,

I think you're man enough to drive Bor—my old boy-friend out of my mind.''

"Does this mean you plan to measure my love-making techniques against his?"

If he only knew the truth, he would have no worries on that score! Lisa thought with irony. "I can assure you, I won't be comparing you to anybody."

"That sounds better." He took a step toward her, then winced. "Blasted ankle."

"Sit!" Lisa grabbed a chair from the small table and pushed it toward him. "You're my patient, re-member?"

"You're not a nurse, remember?" But he lowered himself into it, anyway.

"That doesn't mean I can't take care of you."

"I don't need taking care of."

"The heck you don't! Besides, I need a delaying tactic."

"Because I intimidate you so much?"

"Because, well, I've never done anything like this before," she said as she knelt and began to rub Ry-der's ankle. "I'm not in the habit of picking up men on ski slopes. So lean back and let me get used to touching you."

His chuckle rumbled through her hands, up her arms and all the way to Lisa's core. The sensation thrilled her and frightened her, and she bent quickly to her work.

She couldn't touch the injured area because of the bandage, but Ryder's calf muscles felt tight, so she stroked those. Gradually she felt him relaxing.

It was a heady sensation, to realize this powerful man was yielding himself to her. But, Lisa asked herself uneasily, was she really prepared to give him her virginity?

She felt a flash of anger toward her parents. If they hadn't chosen such an obnoxious husband for her, she *would* have gone to the altar a virgin, which she'd always thought was the right thing to do.

They'd made that impossible by trying to control her. As always.

She had no idea how to open a can of soup because her mother, with the connivance of their chef, had banned her from the kitchen. Her father also kept her on a short leash.

Even when Lisa worked at the company headquarters, her pay had been the unlimited use of a credit card, but no salary. Over the years she'd received cash only to cover incidental expenses.

It was fortunate that she'd stashed enough of that money in her closet in case anything unexpected came up. Like this trip.

Lisa's attention returned to Ryder as her cheek brushed his blue-jeaned leg. It felt firm and well developed. A skier's leg. A man's leg.

She enjoyed kneeling here, massaging him. Acting like a twenty-six-year-old woman instead of a sheltered heiress. Experiencing sensations that her parents wouldn't approve of, with a man they *definitely* wouldn't approve of.

She recalled what Ryder had said, about not wanting people to weigh him down with expectations. It was a good thing he didn't come from a family like hers. Or did he?

"Ryder?" she asked.

"Mmm?" It was a contented murmur.

"Does your family ever make demands on you?" she asked.

"My family?"

"Your parents. Do they push you to get married, or to get a conventional job, that sort of thing?"

A long sigh ran through him. "My dad's gone," he said.

"Gone?" Hoping she wasn't being indelicate, she asked, "You mean...dead?"

"Just gone." Ryder's body tightened, and she resumed massaging his calf. After a moment he leaned back. "Living in the most rundown trailer in the park, having me and my sisters before he was ready, working one odd job after another—he couldn't hack it."

Lisa tried to imagine a life so different from her own and failed. "Weren't there ways he could get ahead? Improve his job skills, that sort of thing?"

A note of bitterness crept into Ryder's voice. "He had the same opportunities as anybody else. But he and Mom never planned ahead. Never postponed anything they wanted, never worked harder than they had to. It was easier to drift...and to drink. Finally Mom threw him out, and we never saw him again."

"What about your mother?" Lisa asked worriedly. "It must have been hard on her."

His tone softened. "She did what she could. Babysitting, housecleaning. Trailer parks can be close communities, and we made a lot of friends there. Then she found another man."

"You didn't like him?"

"He had one thing in common with Dad. He drank," Ryder said. "So she got rid of him, and then along came husband number three, and about that time I joined the Marines."

"What about your sisters?" she asked. "Do you ever see them?"

"We exchange Christmas cards. They're doing all right, I guess." He sounded as if he were tired of the subject, so she dropped it.

Besides, the sense of him that flowed through her hands and into her bloodstream was stirring Lisa past the point of logic. The tangy smell of tomato soup on her blouse also reminded her that it was time to move on.

"I'm ready to shower." She stood up slowly, then indicated the wreckage of the kitchen. "But—"

"The cleaning service comes on Monday. It'll keep till then." Ryder reached for the crutches he'd leaned against the counter. One of them slipped at his touch and crashed to the floor, into a puddle of orangy red. "Wonderful."

"Never mind those." Lisa offered her shoulder for support. "It's not far."

Ryder hesitated. "That isn't necessary."

"It's just to steady your balance."

He paused for another fraction of a second, then said, "Well, let's not make a capital case out of this," and grasped her firmly.

The pressure of his hand set Lisa's shoulder tingling. Heat rolled through her body, tightening her breasts and making her derriere flex instinctively.

As they walked down the hallway, past a small bedroom and bathroom, she didn't feel like the Annalisa she knew, but like someone else. A woman of tender passions and fierce abandon.

Ryder's breathing quickened. As they moved into the master bedroom, he swayed close.

Overhead, a crystal and brass chandelier cast

golden light across the quilted bed, creating a pool of warmth. The door to the bathroom stood open, revealing a bank of mirrors.

Everything was right: the man, the place, the color of the stick in her ovulation kit. She felt clumsy and uncertain, but surely that would pass.

Ryder released her to lean against the interior door frame. As he scorched her with his gaze, Lisa started unworking the buttons on her soiled blouse.

Well, she thought, *here we go into the wild blue yonder.*

Chapter Four

Ryder was by nature a man of action. He considered it his privilege to remove a woman's clothes before making love to her, but Lisa gave one of her fawnlike quivers every time he reached for her, so he stood and watched.

Dark hair curtained her face and shoulders, shielding and revealing her velvet skin as she removed the blouse. She had a fresh, tawny beauty, and the way she exposed it inch by hesitant inch only made her more enticing.

Curving tan lines counterpointed the edges of her bra as she bent to strip away her ski pants. Where had she sunbathed? Ryder mused. Definitely not in Florida, given her mispronunciation of Miami.

Suppressing the urge to rip off his flannel shirt, he eased out of it slowly. Even so, she shot him a startled look as he shrugged free, tossed it aside and reached to unbuckle his belt.

What did the lady expect? For him to take a shower with his clothes on, maybe make love that way?

Then Ryder realized she was still staring at him, drinking in the sight of his bare chest. Surely she'd seen muscular torsos before, and no doubt more sculpted, flamboyant ones than his. At the beach, if not in the bedroom.

Unless, of course, she swam only at a private pool, in restricted company. He was used to putting clues together, and now several of them clicked into place.

She wore expensive clothes. She didn't want to say who she was or where she came from. And, he recalled wryly, she hadn't a clue how to do something as routine as opening a can of soup.

Lisa must be someone's pampered daughter, very pampered. Her slight accent, along with the fact that she couldn't pronounce Miami, indicated she came from a foreign country.

Except for the green eyes, she appeared Hispanic. The name Schmidt could be assumed, or she might have German ancestry. That wouldn't be unusual if she came from certain regions of South America.

"Argentina," he guessed.

Lisa stopped with her pants halfway down her hips. "I beg your pardon?"

"You're from Argentina."

She shook her head.

"Paraguay? Uruguay? Some other 'uay'?"

"I don't understand."

"Who are you?" he said. "Really?"

"Does it matter?" Her frank expression made it clear she didn't want to tell him any more lies, but that she wasn't about to admit the truth, either.

"I want one promise from you," Ryder said.

Gravity pulled her pants the rest of the way to the floor, where they puddled around her feet. In her filmy bra and panties, Lisa stood gazing at him as solemnly as Eve contemplating the apple tree. "What would that be?"

"That this isn't a game. Some kind of rich girl's scavenger hunt." His jaw tightened. "And I'm not your trophy."

"Scavenger hunt?" She regarded him in astonishment. "Do people really do that? Something as intimate as making love, to score points with their friends?"

"Men do," Ryder said. "Or so I've heard. And I have great respect for the ability of women to do anything a man can do. No matter how foolhardy."

Dismay puckered her forehead. "To use someone else for sport! I can't imagine it, Ryder."

She stepped out of her pants and came to stand on tiptoe, one hand reaching to brush his cheek. As their gazes locked, he felt as if they were connecting on several levels at once, plugging into each other's subconscious, infiltrating each other's pasts, opening doors long blocked and throwing windows wide.

Her mouth met his, tentative and light. He let her take the lead, enjoying the sensitivity with which her lips probed his. Then her tongue traced the corners of his mouth and sharp need sliced through his body.

Ryder caught Lisa's waist and pulled her close. Her eyes drifted shut and she melted into him.

He wanted to take her right now. On the floor. In the bed. Anywhere.

And he would have, except that a shift of position sent a wallop of pain roaring through his ankle. A guttural noise wrenched from his throat and he staggered against the door frame.

"Ryder?" Lisa inspected him with concern. "I've hurt you! I'm sorry."

His moan turned to a chuckle. "You, sweetheart,

are pure pleasure. The pain is a whole lot lower down.''

Her glance fell to his ankle. "I forgot." She stepped away, hands fluttering. "What can I do?"

What could she do? He had a ready answer on that score, but the momentum between them had been broken.

If he hadn't felt covered with sweat from the ski slope, and she hadn't been redolent of tomato soup, Ryder might have suggested they put their clothes back on. But, he reminded himself, Lisa needed help to forget the man who had hurt her. He would bring her along gently.

"I could use a little help with these pants," he said.

"As in, getting them off?"

"That's the general idea."

"Will that make your ankle better?" she asked dubiously.

"No, but it will keep my pants dry," he said. "I'd recommend you finish undressing, too. Unless you prefer washing out your underthings while you're still wearing them."

A trace of laughter fleeted across her face. Then, lower lip caught firmly between her teeth, she bent and tugged at his jeans.

WHEN SHE'D CONTEMPLATED losing her virginity, Lisa hadn't given any thought to the details. She had assumed that the man would handle everything.

Apparently matters didn't work that way in real life. Not with this man, anyway.

Awkwardly she fumbled with Ryder's snap. She snatched her hand away when it came into contact with the hard bulge beneath, then forced herself to return to her task as if nothing had happened.

Even through her uneasiness, she wanted him. Her erect nipples strained at the flimsy bra, and a totally unladylike urge kept seizing her to press against him, kiss him, stroke him and make that bulge even larger.

First she had to get his pants off.

Finally the snap popped open. With clumsy fingers, Lisa unzipped him, then knelt and eased the pants around the wrapped ankle.

She pulled them off and stepped back. When she straightened, she got her first good look at the man in his underwear.

Lisa had seen men in skimpy swimsuits, but only at a distance. None of them had come close to the gleaming perfection of Ryder, from his taut jawline down the flat expanse of stomach to his muscled thighs.

A problem occurred to her.

"You don't want to get this bandage wet, do you?" she said.

"I'll stick it out the shower door," he said.

"Won't the water run out?" In her parents' château, a leak on a wooden floor meant lingering dampness and possibly stained plaster on the ceiling below. "It'll make a mess."

"Ever heard of evaporation?" he asked.

The bathroom floor, she saw at a glance, was covered with tile and probably impervious to anything short of a major flood. "Sure," she retorted. "They even have evaporation in Argentina."

"That *is* where you live?"

"They have evaporation everywhere." She

straightened and brushed a cascade of hair from her face.

"You're determined to keep me guessing."

"Not guessing. In the dark."

"Underwear," he said.

She touched the elastic around her hips.

"Mine."

Lisa shook her head. "You can remove your own."

"But I'm in such terrible pain," he deadpanned. Only the glint in his eyes gave him away.

"I think you're faking this whole injury."

"I wish I were." He let out an exaggerated sigh and folded his arms. He watched her, wolflike in his stillness.

"In a minute," she said.

"Take your time."

As she unhooked her bra, she felt his scrutiny fix on her breasts. With deliberate motions, she slid down her panties and stepped out of them, and heard a soft, involuntary whistle.

Crouching in front of Ryder, Lisa looked away as she reached for his waist and pulled down the wisp of cotton. She moved back quickly.

He didn't stir, but she could sense tension rippling beneath the surface. When she dared to look, she saw that he was unabashedly ready. Very ready.

Intense curiosity gripped Lisa. She wanted to unleash the feral hunger that lurked beneath his iron self-control. She wanted to experience this man with every part of herself.

Her breasts felt full. Swollen, aching to be caressed. If only she could bring herself to approach him.

Ryder turned away, into the bathroom. The stiffness of his back betrayed how tightly he was holding himself in check.

In his restraint, she perceived the man his résumé had described. An ex-Marine. A former police detective. A hard man, an experienced one. She needed all that experience, but the hardness frightened her a little.

The shower burst into life, echoing off the walls and filling the bathroom with a rushing noise. The air grew misty.

Ryder hobbled into the vertical stall, leaving the frosted glass door open wide enough to accommodate his bandaged ankle. "We should put a plastic bag over it," he said. "Got one handy?"

Lisa shook her head.

"Then you'd better come scrub me in a hurry."

She grabbed a washcloth off the rack. She had helped scrub down one of Nicola's show horses, back before her friend's divorce. This shouldn't be any harder, should it?

"You've got the strangest expression on your face," Ryder said.

"I do?"

"Steely determination." His eyes narrowed in contemplation. "Afraid of catching a hoof in your side?"

"How did you know?" she asked in amazement.

"Rich girls always have horses," he said.

"They weren't mine! They were the baron's!" She stopped in dismay, halfway into the stall. How much had she revealed? There were a lot of barons in the world, weren't there?

"The baron?" Ryder shook his head. "This creepy ex-boyfriend of yours was a baron?"

Water sprayed her face, and she realized it must be

drenching the bathroom. Lisa hustled inside and closed the glass door as far as she could.

"It was a nickname," she protested, and knew instantly he didn't believe her.

"As far as I know, they don't have barons in Argentina." Ryder propped one elbow on an oversize soap tray for support. He gave off a spicy male scent, rich with exertion and laced with subliminal allure. "Europe, then. Your name's Schmidt, so you're from Austria? Germany?"

"Would you like to see my lederhosen?"

"Some other time."

Lisa snatched up the bar of soap and rubbed it across the washcloth. As briskly as possible, she polished Ryder's chest and shoulders.

A large hand clamped onto her arm, and Ryder removed the cloth. "No, Lisa," he said. "Let me show you how it's done."

"You don't have to," she gulped. "I can try it again."

He started to laugh. "Were you this uptight with the baron?"

"No! Yes!" She wasn't sure what she wanted him to believe.

Retracting his leg through the door, and heedless of the water drenching the bandage, he pinned her against the fiberglass wall. "Stop wiggling or I'll never get you clean."

"Your wrapping! It'll be soaked!"

"We can do it over. There must be a first aid kit around here somewhere."

He bent over Lisa, large and powerful. She wanted to squirm away, but there was no room. Anyway, the soapy cloth was swishing across her neck and shoulders so gently that she began to calm.

"Step away from the wall. So I can get your back," he murmured.

At least she wouldn't have to face him anymore. "I'll turn—"

"No, you won't." Standing in front, he reached around Lisa and stroked her back with the nubbly cloth.

She couldn't help bumping into him, her naked flesh rubbing his. When she did, he held her tightly in place, so that she felt the whole man along the length of her body.

His legs were corded and lightly furred. His chest and upper arms had turned slick, and his hair smelled of herbal shampoo.

She was still registering her impressions when his hand on her elbow turned her slightly, and Ryder washed her side, then adjusted her so he could reach the other one. "You've done this before," she accused. "What was all that nonsense about being monastic?"

"I've never done this, exactly," he said. "But I used to wash the family dog."

"I beg your pardon!"

He chuckled at her indignation. "Rich girls have horses. Kids who live in trailers have dogs."

"I remind you of washing your pet?" she sputtered.

"Trust me, it wasn't nearly this much fun," he said, and drew the washcloth along the valley between her breasts.

The sensation was so intense that Lisa gasped. Ryder's lips quirked with satisfaction at her reaction, and then, bracing one hand against the fiberglass, he bent and caught one nipple between his lips.

Pure agonizing desire wiped her mind and spirit clean. The sensation that licked through her was a flame, swiftly roaring into a fire.

Lisa's hand cupped the back of Ryder's head, holding him against her and urging him on. He released the nipple and moved to the other one.

Her back arched instinctively, and her free hand moved along his hips. He shifted back and forth between her breasts until heat suffused her, and steam seemed to rise directly from their skin.

To her astonishment Lisa felt no shyness at all. No hesitancy as he pressed tighter against her.

She wanted this. Needed it. Ached for it. When he lifted his head to study her, she caught his mouth with hers and yielded to the acute urge to press against him.

Strong fingers caught her buttocks. He was groaning, low and deep, and then suddenly, painfully, he drew away.

"What's wrong?" she rasped. "Is it your foot?"

He shook his head, spraying droplets of water around the stall. "I forgot about protection."

"What?"

"I've got to find some—there must be a condom somewhere in this house." He uttered a low oath, then apologized. "It's frustrating, that's all."

A condom? Ryder wanted to use a condom?

Lisa couldn't believe it. She might lose her virginity with no chance of getting pregnant?

She would never find another man like him. A clean medical slate, character references and—

So intense. So sensual. His bronzed skin gleaming in the shower.

She needed to change the subject in a hurry. Brushing a wet strand of hair from Ryder's temple, she fingered a jagged white line above it. "How did you get this scar?"

"A Marine rescue operation," he said. "There was a revolution in—well, central Africa. They've changed the name of the country since then. We had to go in and pull out the American citizens."

"You got shot?" she asked.

"Potted."

"What?"

"Somebody threw a pot at me," he said. "Whacked me right there. I was so dazed, I still had the pot in my hand when I got onto the helicopter."

"What kind of pot?" she asked.

"Teapot," he said.

"Did everyone get out safely?"

"Heck, yes," he said.

"You were a hero then, too."

"They would have been okay, anyway," he said. "The revolution was over by the time we landed."

Lisa started to laugh. "You make it sound so casual."

Ryder watched her with amused fascination. "You're lovely when you laugh. I shouldn't tell you that, though."

"Why not?"

"Gives you too much power," he murmured.

"You're the one with the power," she said, and drew his hips against hers.

Until that moment, Lisa had tried not to think about

what she was doing. Now, she couldn't not think about it.

Because, in that instant, she knew that she was incomplete and would never be whole unless she possessed Ryder. Unless they coupled, mated, filled each other. It was more than an urge or a need. It was a compulsion.

She could feel the change in him, too. His hips moved in a rhythm of their own, while the arms encircling her waist hardened into a viselike grip. There could be no more space between them, anywhere.

In a blur of spattering water and with a few stifled expletives when Ryder put too much weight on his ankle, they shifted out of the shower stall onto a fluffy bath rug. The contrast in textures between wet and dry, cold air and stray drops of hot water, faded before the all-encompassing yearning that only Ryder could satisfy.

Lisa yielded to an elemental force that was partly herself and partly this man. She stroked him everywhere, with every part of her body, and opened herself to him without reserve.

He entered her with a long, pulsing stroke. There was a momentary twinge, and then he plunged all the way in. Lisa cried out and kneaded his back, wanting more but not knowing what more there could be.

Lifting himself on his elbows, Ryder withdrew. As warm water dripped from his skin to hers, Lisa heard him suck in a harsh breath.

She didn't feel finished. Yet they'd had intercourse, hadn't they? She was no longer a virgin.

"Ryder?" she whispered.

"I don't want this to go too fast." A line furrowed his forehead. "Were you— Did I imagine—"

She passed one hand along his bare hip and felt him shiver. Curving against him, she discovered he was still hard.

There *was* more. There had to be, because if he didn't take her again, she would explode into a ball of steam.

"Kiss me," she said.

"Like this?" His lips caught hers, almost roughly. She could feel the teeth behind them, the wolflike ferocity. "Or this?" As his tongue invaded her mouth, he drove between her legs and held her pinioned.

Lisa had never been so close to delirium. She wanted everything at once, and yet she was completely in his power.

He began to thrust slowly into her body...and at the same slow tempo, explored her mouth with his tongue.

She writhed against Ryder and knew a keen joy when he responded with swifter movements. The joy heightened and concentrated into almost unbearable pleasure. Wildness engulfed her.

She rode a crest of fireworks, sizzling and snapping with impossibly pure crimsons and golds. Lisa clung to Ryder as if they might both rocket off the face of the earth and felt his entire being vibrate in response. He called her name, over and over, and somehow that sound, deep and ragged, brought them both safely to earth.

She lay in the glow of his arms, vaguely aware of a wet rug beneath them and the thrum of the shower a few feet away. So this, she thought, was how babies got made. The only wonder was that every square foot of the earth hadn't been filled with children eons ago.

Ryder let out a contented sigh as he withdrew from her. Lisa wondered if there were a delicate way to ask him how soon they could do this again.

He untangled his legs and scooted back. Several inches, but it felt like miles.

"Why didn't you tell me you were a virgin?" he said.

Chapter Five

Ryder waited for Lisa to tell another lie. He couldn't imagine how she could even come up with a convincing truth for giving a stranger her virginity, let alone cover it with a fabrication.

Too edgy to hold still, he gripped the edge of the counter, pulled himself up and limped over to finish showering. When he emerged, he surveyed Lisa as she sat brooding in a tangle of black hair and olive skin.

If only she weren't so impossibly beautiful, he might be able to think straight. No doubt she found it easy to manipulate people, he reflected unhappily. The way she'd apparently done with him. "Well?"

"I didn't tell you because I didn't want you to know," she said. "How often can people do that?"

"Do what?"

"What we just did. Have sex," she said. "Do we have to wait an hour or something?"

"You mean like swimming after eating?" He shook his head. "Lady, I'm not about to get sidetracked. Why on earth would you pick a stranger to—" Another complication struck him. "We didn't even use protection. These days, heaven knows what risks you ran.''

Despite the wet floor, she rose gracefully. Like a nymph, he thought, and could have punched himself for such a ridiculous notion.

''I took your medical history, remember?'' She reached for a white towel.

''I could have lied.''

''Why would you? You thought I was a nurse.''

''Because, although I suppose you already know this, some people lie all the time.'' Ryder winced as his ankle, which had been behaving itself, resumed throbbing. He held tight to the edge of the shower stall, but refused to make any further concessions to weakness. ''They like being in control, and keeping other people in the dark is one way to accomplish that.''

Lisa stopped in the act of wrapping the towel around her waist, sarong-style. ''You mean me?''

''You see anybody else around here who's stretched the truth like bubble gum?''

''I haven't stretched anything. I lied outright.'' The white terry cloth brought out the olive of her skin, and, infuriatingly, she had left herself naked from the waist up. Against his will, Ryder's body began to come alive again.

''Lisa! Answer my question!''

''There is a man I'm trying to escape from, but he isn't a baron,'' she said.

''And—let's see—he'll leave you alone if you can prove you aren't a virgin?'' Ryder said.

''Well, no.''

He was glad she hadn't seized on that obvious pretext. ''You just wanted to find out what sex was like before you shackled yourself to someone, let's see, rich and powerful and acceptable to your parents?''

"Absolutely not!" Her eyes flashed green fire. "I don't want to marry him at all."

"Well, I have good news for you—you don't have to." Ryder grabbed a blue towel and yanked it around his own midsection. "We have a slogan in this country. It's called Just Say No."

He stuck the end of the towel into place and lifted his hands. With scarcely a slither of warning, the terry cloth dropped to the floor.

"You didn't pull it tight enough," said Lisa.

"Maybe you could show me."

She quirked one eyebrow. "I'd be happy to. But you haven't answered *my* question."

"What question was that?"

"How long do we have to wait before we do it again?"

He couldn't believe her nerve. Worse, the longer he stared at her bare breasts and lively face, the quicker his body was getting ready for a rematch. In his present state of undress, that fact would soon be all too obvious.

"Decades," he said, and hobbled out of the bathroom.

She followed on his tail. "Are you angry?"

He tried to snatch his clothes off the floor and managed to twist his ankle painfully. "Pick that up for me, will you?"

Lisa scooped up the garments, scarcely seeming aware that she was still half-nude. Ryder took the chance to examine her breasts with more objectivity than had been previously possible and decided they were perfect.

"My girlfriends told me that guys like to have sex," she said as she handed them over. "I didn't think you would mind, you know, doing it."

"That wasn't the part I'm objecting to." He removed the soggy bandages from his ankle, tossed them to her and dressed quickly. "It's the other part."

"The, uh, fib?" said Lisa.

"Fibs, plural." He finished pulling up his jeans. "Poke around in the medicine chest and see if you can find a first aid kit, will you?" It occurred to Ryder that she might not know what one looked like. "It should be a white box with a red cross on it."

With a rueful nod, she vanished back into the bathroom.

"If it's not in the cabinet, try under the sink!"

As rustling and clicking sounds emerged, Ryder did what any other red-blooded American private investigator would do. He went into the living room and opened Lisa's purse.

It was simply but artfully styled of soft gray leather. There was no designer name to be seen, which showed it must be *really* exclusive.

He examined the contents: a miniature silver comb and brush; a metallic makeup kit of museum-quality design; a small vial of perfume from which wafted the scents of springtime and mystery.

Upon opening the sleek wallet, he let out a low whistle. It contained $2,389 in American money plus miscellaneous change. No foreign coins. No credit cards. There was an international driver's license in the name of Lisa Schmidt, with an address in Zurich.

Switzerland? He hadn't thought of that.

Beneath the wallet lay a Swiss passport. This, Ryder decided, was finally getting him somewhere. Inside she was identified, once again, as Lisa Schmidt. The passport had been stamped only once, yesterday, at JFK International in New York.

That was odd. Miss Lisa Schmidt might have left her foreign money and credit cards in her hotel room, but it was quite a coincidence that she had come to America with a brand-new, never-before-used passport.

Unless, of course, it was a fake.

This whole situation was getting stranger by the minute. Somebody could be setting Ryder up, but what did they intend to do, blackmail him? He wasn't married or a politician, and as far as he knew, deflowering a virgin by mutual consent was no crime.

Maybe one of the men he'd captured over the years hoped to hurt him. But how? They couldn't have known, he reflected as he returned Lisa's papers to her purse, that she would awaken feelings he hadn't known he was capable of.

Like tenderness. And protectiveness. And an irrational wish that she would stick around for a while.

"Ryder?" Lisa, still half-naked, stood radiating anxiety as she watched him replace her purse on the coffee table. "What are you doing?"

"I wish I knew what a real Swiss passport looks like," he said. "I could find out."

"Do you care?" Her eyes had gone wide and vulnerable. Her hands clamped onto the first aid kit so tightly, he feared the thing might crack.

"Are you working for someone?"

"No."

"Do you have an ulterior motive?"

"Yes, but it doesn't concern you."

"Excuse me?" If he could bottle the sincerity in

those emerald eyes, Ryder reflected, he could make a million dollars as a con man.

"Did you ever want something in your life to be flawless? Just once, so you could hold it in your memory forever?" As she spoke, Lisa sat on the coffee table, opened the first aid kit and pried the cover off a roll of bandages.

"No." Ryder plopped his leg on the coffee table without much grace. The thud sent needles of agony shooting through his ankle.

"I guess you wouldn't need to, because you can keep searching for whatever you want until you find it," she went on as she placed his ankle firmly in her lap and began wrapping it. "But my life isn't usually within my own control. However, this one thing, this first time, I wanted to have my way."

"I should be honored that I was chosen to deflower you?" Ryder growled, trying to ignore the scent of flowers wafting from her hair. "Without my prior knowledge or consent, I might add."

Lisa worked along with smooth proficiency. "I apologize. I thought you would simply enjoy having sex and wouldn't care why you got it."

Her explanation for her behavior almost rang true. But Ryder was not the sort of man to be satisfied with "almost," particularly when other discrepancies kept cropping up. "How is it that you can wrap an ankle like an expert when you couldn't even open a can of soup?"

"I did volunteer work at a hospital," Lisa said. "It was the only activity my parents would allow." Expertly she ripped off the end of the bandage and fixed it in place with two strips of adhesive. "There!"

"Good as new," he grumbled.

She put away the bandages and shut the kit. "Ryder, make love to me again."

"Why? Wasn't that perfect enough?"

She laughed. "Too perfect. I want more."

"But not enough to stick around very long." He wondered why he'd said that. Ryder didn't *want* anybody sticking around.

"Does it matter?" she asked. "Won't you take me the way I am?"

Oh, yes, he would. He wanted to take her in every way possible, in every conceivable position. On the couch. On the floor. In the kitchen—no, scratch that, it was still a mess.

"Come here," he said. "Let's see if we can't make it just a little more perfect.

LISA HAD NEVER KNOWN there could be such pleasure in the world. And it wasn't only physical.

She had never suspected that she would want to yield to a man so completely, nor that he could also yield to her. Ryder had a way of holding her, of gazing at her, of teasing her, that exceeded even her dreams.

As they dozed side by side later that evening, she admitted silently that this discovery of what could happen between a man and a woman was completely unexpected. Could she give it up, now that she had found it?

Pensively, Lisa studied the man in bed with her. He lay amid rumpled covers, with one arm thrown across his forehead. Shadows and moonlight brought out the classic lines of his cheeks and nose.

Suppose she did have Ryder's baby. Was it fair that

he would never know his child? Or that the child would never have a father?

What if it resembled him so strongly that, every day for the next twenty years, Lisa found herself staring into searching brown eyes, a reminder of her deception and of this brief happiness? What if she spent the rest of her life wishing she'd never left Ryder?

Maybe she shouldn't.

She caught her breath. She'd never had such a rebellious thought before in her life.

Scarcely daring to believe what she was considering, she assessed the ramifications. It would be wrong to disappear, leaving her parents distraught. But, as Ryder had said, Lisa did have the freedom to reject their choice of a husband and to live her own way.

With him? Would that be possible?

He was different from anyone she had known. Her parents would never accept him, but then, he would probably never accept them, either.

The prospect of disappointing her family wrenched at Lisa. She wouldn't do it just for her own selfish pleasure.

Still, as Ryder had made clear, he was no object to be used and discarded. Unintentionally or not, a chain of events beyond his control had brought her into his world and perhaps started his baby growing inside her. If he had truly fallen in love, he had a claim on her equal to that of her parents.

Her return flight to Paris departed New York late Monday. In order to catch it, she would have to leave here early that morning, the day after tomorrow.

She had one day, Sunday, to decide the course of her future. Not a long time to assess his true feelings or hers, but it would have to do.

With a sense of infinite danger and possibilities, Lisa ran her hand down Ryder's shoulder and across his chest. Stirring in his sleep, he gave a contented sigh.

Lover. Husband. Life's companion. Was it possible? She could scarcely wait to find out.

BORIS COULD NOT BELIEVE his bad luck. A private card game with a group of Japanese businessmen had sounded like easy pickings.

It had been—for them. They had peeled him like a banana. Why hadn't someone told him they were Yakuza? Now he was in debt to two sets of gangsters.

Then Lothaire called to say that Miss De La Pena, using the name Lisa Schmidt, had caught a connecting flight to Denver, rented a car and disappeared.

"There has to be some record of where she is!" Boris snapped. "Find it!"

"No further credit charges from America have been posted, but I have made a few discoveries," Lothaire replied coolly. Despite his youth, he was rarely disconcerted by Boris's bad temper. "Prior to her departure, she received a package from Geneva. The return address was that of Win Hoffer, the cameraman who shot your video."

"What?" Boris could make no sense of this.

"The maid believes that his girlfriend, a Canadian woman, is a friend of Miss De La Pena," Lothaire continued smoothly.

"What was in the package?"

"A fashion magazine," he said. "That is all she saw. But also, Miss De La Pena went to a pharmacy near the château, and afterward the maid saw an ovulation kit in her bathroom."

"An ovulation kit?" Boris knew nothing about such female devices. "What does it mean?"

"I will contact Mr. Hoffer," said Lothaire. "For a price I think he will tell us anything he knows. Also, I have learned the flight on which the young lady will be returning from New York. It departs on Monday night."

"Let's hope she's on it," snarled Boris.

"I do not believe in hope," said Lothaire. "I believe in preparation."

"That's why I pay you." In the silence that followed, Boris recalled that Lothaire's last paycheck had bounced. "Of course, I will make good on your back wages."

"I know you will," said his employee. "Once we have Miss De La Pena in hand."

Boris liked the sound of that. As he broke the connection, he felt almost cheerful, until he remembered that he had just lost over a hundred thousand dollars to the Japanese mob.

"NO, SIR, MS. SCHMIDT hasn't made any phone calls," the hotel clerk said. "There are no additional charges to her bill."

Phone calls would have meant phone numbers, which could be helpful in pinpointing Lisa's true identity, if Ryder ever needed to. Failing that, he wouldn't mind a peek at her credit card number. "Would you please get the tab ready for her to sign?"

"It's already been taken care of," said the clerk.

"Thanks." Giving the counter a frustrated smack, Ryder limped across the lobby. It was busy for a Sunday, with some tourists heading to the ski slopes and others wandering into the dining room for brunch.

Already this morning he and Lisa had returned his crutches to the ski lodge and accepted an employee's offer to drop off his car at the chalet. The fact that such helpfulness was probably motivated by the desire to avoid a lawsuit over his "accident" didn't make it any less convenient.

Once at the hotel, Lisa had gone upstairs to collect her possessions to take to the chalet. Now Ryder waited impatiently as the minutes ticked by.

Across the lobby, an elevator door swished open and a middle-aged couple got out. Seeing no one else, he felt a jolt of concern.

Where was Lisa? Had she sneaked out while he was waiting? He wished he didn't care so much. He also wished he didn't feel so uncertain of her intentions.

A second elevator opened. And then there she was, pulling a wheeled suitcase as she marched across the floor in high-heeled boots.

In spite of himself, relief rushed through Ryder. In the blink of an eye, it was replaced by appreciation.

The soiled ski outfit had been replaced by a fuzzy pink sweater over white silk slacks. It was an utterly impractical outfit for doing anything except...

Well, except having her garments stripped off, which was exactly what he longed to do. But he wanted much more of Lisa than she had given him so far, and the only way to get it was to leave her body alone for a while.

"Allow me." He hobbled forward and reached for the suitcase. After a moment's pause, she gave it to him.

"This won't take a sec." Her mane of dark hair

shifting around her, Lisa floated across the lobby and presented her key to the clerk.

The young man stopped chattering on the phone and stared at her for a long second before saying something that looked to Ryder like, "Thank you. Please come back. And I really mean that."

On her return trip across the lobby, Lisa turned the heads of an old man reading a newspaper, a bell captain loading luggage onto a cart and a teenage boy following his parents toward the dining room. She didn't appear to notice that they all wore the same deer-in-the-headlights expression.

No wonder. Ryder supposed he was wearing it himself.

His ankle throbbing at every step, he managed with all the grace of a moose in a mudhole to get himself and the suitcase out the door and alongside Lisa's rental car. Straining to lift the heavy bag into the trunk while balancing on his one good leg, he was relieved to see the doorman hurrying toward him.

"Let me help you, miss!" Ignoring Ryder, the man rushed ahead of Lisa and held the driver's door for her. "May I say it's been a pleasure serving you?"

She smiled and gave him a tip. To Ryder's amazement, the man actually hesitated as if reluctant to accept money from her. In the end he pocketed it and sauntered back to his post, whistling.

Grumpily, Ryder finished stuffing the suitcase into the trunk, slammed it and got into the passenger seat. His bad mood made no sense to him, unless he was jealous, and that possibility made him even grumpier.

"Turn right at the next corner," he said.

Lisa turned on the ignition and eased the car forward.

"The chalet's to the left."

"We need to do a little shopping."

The last thing Ryder wanted was to put any more stress on his ankle, but they couldn't go on as they had been. Lisa might be naive enough not to worry about pregnancy, but he wasn't.

"Turn here," he said when they reached the supermarket-pharmacy.

"We're buying groceries?"

"That, too," he said.

She didn't follow his drift until they arrived at the display of condoms. Thin ones, textured ones, blue ones, even packages with tattoo-style images on them.

"Do you have a preference?" he said.

Her mouthed opened and closed, and she swallowed hard. For heaven's sake, what was bothering her? And why did the young man in the next aisle have to stare at her with such puppylike adoration?

"I, uh, I think I'm allergic to—that stuff," she said.

"How would you know?"

"At the hospital. We had to wear gloves, and they made me break out."

At the end of the aisle, the young man crashed his cart into a shelf of feminine hygiene products, sending pink-wrapped packets flying across the linoleum. Lisa didn't notice.

"Rubber gloves or plastic ones?"

"I don't remember."

"Maybe they've got something hypoallergenic." Ryder poked through the rack until he spotted a package marked "For Sensitive Skin." "This ought to do it."

Lisa nodded mutely. The young man, his face scarlet as he shoved fallen products back onto the shelf, watched with longing as she and Ryder walked off.

In the grocery section, the cart quickly filled with supplies. Salmon filets, the makings of cream sauce with capers, crisp butterhead lettuce, tomatoes, croutons, blue cheese dressing, baked potatoes large enough to stuff and cheddar cheese to stuff them with.

"Isn't that a lot of food?" Lisa asked dubiously as they headed for the checkout. "Won't it take hours to fix?"

"Sure," said Ryder. "We've got all day, haven't we?"

With his peripheral vision, he spotted the clumsy young man heading for the same checkout stand, trying to angle ahead of them through the clutter of promotional displays. Ryder sped up, despite a protesting twinge from his ankle.

Lisa kept pace easily. "I never thought of cooking with a man," she said. "What a lovely idea."

"We'll have to clean the kitchen first." From the side, the young man was racewalking toward the checkout stand, about to cut them off. "You're not exactly dressed for it."

"Then I'll have to undress for it," Lisa responded a bit more loudly than he might have wished.

A *crash* made them both flinch. Videotapes flew every which way, and shoppers turned to stare at the overturned display table and the young man whose face was nearing a terminal shade of purple.

Whistling under his breath, Ryder made his way to the counter and began unloading his purchases.

Chapter Six

"She intends to get pregnant?" Boris clamped the cellular phone tighter against his ear. He would never have believed the spoiled young heiress capable of such duplicity! "Does she think that would stop me from marrying her?"

"She believes that what her parents really want is an heir, not a son-in-law," responded Lothaire's voice.

"It is absurd! Are you sure you have the right girl?"

"Win himself arranged for her fake passport, through friends who import his film supplies. She is using the name Lisa Schmidt."

"But he doesn't know who she was seeing in Denver?"

"He claims not to know of anyone in the entire state of Colorado," said Lothaire. "Apparently she made the contact herself. A resourceful girl, this Miss De La Pena."

Boris wished he had his hands on Annalisa's resources right now. Or, failing that, on her neck.

Furiously he jerked the leather-covered steering wheel, which was not a good idea at 120 kilometers per hour on the Autobahn. The car swerved and he nearly dropped the phone before he got back on course.

"Mr. Grissofsky?"

"Here!" he snapped. "What else have you found out?"

"She has a flight from Denver that arrives in New York Monday afternoon."

"So what? We already know she's leaving for Paris that night."

"She arrives at LaGuardia Airport," Lothaire went on as if he hadn't heard. "To catch her plane to Paris, she must take a taxi from LaGuardia to JFK. This is the point at which she will be most vulnerable."

"Vulnerable to what?"

"I am flying to New York today," Lothaire continued in his maddeningly level voice. "I will arrive in time to make certain arrangements. I suggest you meet me there as soon as possible."

"In New York?" Despite the turmoil in his brain, which had risen to near panic levels in recent days, Boris recalled that cellular phone conversations were easily intercepted by eavesdroppers. Certain things could not be said, but what *was* Lothaire getting at? "As you know, I came to Germany to close a lucrative deal. There is no way—"

"This marriage, Mr. Grissofsky, is the deal of a lifetime," his associate reminded him.

"I hardly think the sight of me will inspire Miss De La Pena to abandon her baby scheme!"

"Miss De La Pena will not see you. *I* will be driving the cab," said Lothaire.

"What cab?"

"The one she will catch at LaGuardia."

Finally Lothaire's drift came clear. They were going to kidnap the heiress! No doubt the young man would arrange to have a suitable drug on hand to subdue her and a chartered plane waiting on a nearby runway.

"Do you have a destination in mind?" Boris asked.

"A Caribbean island that I would prefer not to name over the phone," said Lothaire. "There is no waiting for marriage ceremonies, and no questions asked."

In the year and a half since the young man had come to work for him, Boris had learned to rely on him absolutely. "Very good."

The German deal would have to be postponed. It was a shame, because it involved black market trading, which meant off-the-books profits free of taxes and duties.

On the other hand, Boris suspected that his would-be partners were ex-members of the Stasi. If he ended up in debt to them, he would have the Yakuza, the Russian mob *and* the former East German secret police on his tail. He wasn't sure even the prospect of Annalisa Schmidt De La Pena's vast inheritance would be enough to stave off all of them.

"I'll meet you wherever you like," he said.

SOMEWHERE BETWEEN making caper sauce and watching Lisa gyrate to the New Orleans-style zydeco music on the CD player, Ryder realized he was falling in love.

Hopelessly. Stupidly. With a woman he knew he shouldn't trust and yet somehow did.

During the course of the afternoon, she had drawn him out about his childhood and his struggle to make his own way in the world. Every bit of information seemed to fascinate her.

The only things he'd learned about Miss Lisa Schmidt were that she came from Switzerland and had rich, overprotective parents.

And yet...

Clad in a beige apron with a teddy bear stitched on the front, she had pitched in cheerfully to clean and cook. Despite her inexperience, she followed directions intelligently and found ways to make the process more efficient.

If he didn't know better, Ryder might have said she had executive ability. Then, every once in a while, he would see a flash of innocence, just enough to throw him off guard and dig the fishhook deeper into his heart.

She was reeling him in. He wondered why he didn't mind.

At last the potatoes were in the oven, the caper sauce ready for the final touches, and the salad cooling in the refrigerator. They wouldn't be able to finish their work for another hour.

Lisa hung her apron in the pantry and swung toward him. "What now?"

Ryder refrained from suggesting they take another shower, or skip the shower altogether. He wanted to learn more about her, and that required staying *out* of bed.

"How about a glass of something?" He indicated the wine rack. This morning, after confirming Joe Ortiz's capture, he'd wired Nina McNally a bouquet with the good news. The widow had phoned to thank him and to urge that he enjoy a bottle of her wine in celebration.

Lisa shook her head. "It's all domestic. I only drink French." She wrinkled her nose. "I'm sorry. That sounded snobbish."

Ryder studied her, bemused and torn. "I was impressed because it's good stuff from California. I keep forgetting how different we are."

She laid one hand on his arm. "Surely every couple has different tastes and experiences that have to be worked out. After all, how many people these days marry the boy next door?"

The word *marry* made his breath catch in his throat. Ryder didn't know whether he felt alarm over the possibility of being tied down, or relief that she might consider staying.

The image of his parents' rundown home, of jobs that led nowhere and children who always needed new shoes lurked at the back of Ryder's mind. It had motivated him to survive boot camp, to be the hardest-working cop on the force and to stay blessedly and permanently single.

But would it be so terrible to have a woman like Lisa to come home to? Or travel with, when his work wasn't too dangerous?

Cooking with her had been fun, not a chore. He could hardly wait to introduce Lisa to the rest of his life: dancing at nightclubs, barbecuing at the beach, attending the oddball festivals that popped up nearly every weekend somewhere in Southern California. She brought such zest to everything she did, he knew it would be a pleasure just watching her go through life.

A woman like her could open new horizons to him as well, Ryder mused as he uncorked a bottle of cabernet sauvignon. He was curious about art and dance, foreign films and classical music, but he had a healthy dislike for making a fool of himself. What he needed was a guide. Possibly even someone like Lisa, who had mentioned that she and her mother enjoyed attending the theater.

As he found two wineglasses in the cupboard and filled them, Ryder began to hum. He didn't want to be tied down; that hadn't changed. But until today, it had never occurred to him that a relationship might set him free instead.

He handed a glass to Lisa. She sniffed it, then sipped. "It's good."

"You're just saying that."

She frowned. "It *is* good. I never joke about wine." Picking up the bottle, she studied the label. "It's from the Napa Valley. I've heard of that, but I don't know this particular winery. Well, live and learn."

He lifted his glass. "To living and learning."

They clinked, and drank. It was, Ryder thought with uncharacteristic hopefulness, a beginning.

BY HER SECOND GLASS of wine Lisa began to feel a bit too relaxed. Having grown up in a culture where imbibing was considered a normal part of dining, she didn't take into account, until nearly too late, the fact that she was drinking on an empty stomach.

She set her third glass on the coffee table, untasted. "I'll save that for later."

They were stretched on the couch, Lisa nestled between Ryder's legs and reclining back against him. "Tell me more about Switzerland," he murmured from behind.

The casual intimacy of their position, and the buzz

from the wine, made her chatty. "It's beautiful. Spectacular mountains and picture-postcard villages. Like the cliché says, the Swiss are very clean and as orderly as clockwork."

"You said 'The Swiss,' not 'we,'" he observed, his baritone voice vibrating into her spine.

Oops. "My family has several homes." Lisa paused, reluctant to juggle any more half-truths. She ached instead to melt into Ryder until they understood each other by osmosis.

"Several homes," he repeated. "As in mansions?"

"In Paris, we have an apartment," Lisa said. "It's fairly spacious, if you count the servants' rooms."

"You'd have a hard time adjusting to my place in L.A. I have a one-bedroom apartment that makes this chalet look like the Taj Mahal."

There was a question behind the statement, and even in her mellow state she caught it. He was checking to see if she would consider staying there with him. Lisa's heart swelled at the implication.

"I'd rather have a small place where I could feel at home, than a castle where I'm treated like a prisoner," she said.

His grip tightened around her. "That's how your parents treat you?"

"Sometimes."

"Then you aren't going back," he said.

You aren't going back. The words echoed happily in her mind.

She wanted to ask what he meant, but Lisa realized he'd made the remark without considering its implications. Her judgment warned her not to rely on impulsive words. All the same, she felt like singing and dancing.

Instead she closed her eyes, blotting out the sunlight that streamed through the blue-and-white room. Now the only thing she sensed was Ryder: his musky aroma, the heat from his chest, the beating of his heart.

He pulled her more snugly against him, and she felt him harden. Lisa wondered if people could make love in this position and hoped she was about to find out.

A timer went off in the kitchen. Its insistent *beep-beep* broke the spell, and reluctantly she scooted forward.

"Time for round two in the kitchen." Ruefully Ryder swung to his feet and helped her up.

He retrieved the potatoes from the oven with tongs. "They need to cool before we can scoop them out and stuff them," he said. "The salmon won't take long to broil, and the sauce just needs to be heated."

"So we've got a little time?" Lisa said.

"Did you have something specific in mind?" He arched an eyebrow.

"When you're around, it's hard to think about anything else," she confessed. Seeing his half amused, half dubious expression, she explained, "I like holding you. I like watching your reactions to me. Most of all, I like it when you lose control."

"That appeals to you, does it?" he teased.

"Maybe it's because you're so strong and self-contained. When you open up and let me inside, it means something special."

Lisa wasn't sure it was wise to speak so frankly; Nicola had advised her to keep men guessing. But then, Nicola hadn't had much luck finding the man of her dreams.

"When you let me inside, it means something special to me, too." This time, he hadn't blurted the words: he meant what he was saying.

No longer skittish around him, Lisa crossed the floor and placed her hands on Ryder's shoulders. Although she was tall, he rose a good six inches above her.

He lowered his head slowly, gauging her reaction, delaying until at last their lips met. Then he caught her hips and drew her against him.

When the kiss ended, he gazed at her for a long moment. "You belong to me. Not like a possession. But I feel as if we fit together."

"I know." Lisa, usually so ready with words, could find nothing eloquent to add, so she said, "Are we going to stand here shooting the breeze all day?"

With a whoop, Ryder caught her waist and started to hoist her into his arms. Abruptly, he staggered, and they nearly crashed into the door frame. "Damn! I forgot about the ankle!"

"Let me rub it."

"You can rub anything you like."

They went into the bedroom arm in arm, stopping in the doorway for another kiss. "Let's postpone the rubbing," said Lisa.

"Of my ankle, anyway," he agreed.

"The way we were sitting on the couch..."

"You want to try that?"

"Could we?"

"I'd like nothing better." He led her to the bed, sat on the edge and reached for her. When she leaned over him, deft hands unworked her slacks, lifted the fuzzy pink sweater and unhooked her bra.

His mouth closed over one erect nipple, while he

cradled both breasts. Feverishly Lisa buried her face in his hair, wanting so many things at once that she could scarcely sort them out.

They eased onto the bed. Her pants slid down her hips, and she kicked them off.

She unbuttoned Ryder's shirt and knelt above him, bending to trace a line down the center of his chest with her tongue. He tasted of salt and desire.

A moan welled from his throat. Beneath her fingers, the bulge in his pants assumed massive proportions.

A tug at his buckle freed the belt, and Lisa helped him shed his jeans. Her sweater and panties joined his underpants on the floor.

Would he remember the condoms? The unwelcome thought cooled her for a fraction of a second, and then Ryder propped himself against the pillows and pulled her backward on top of him.

"This was the way you wanted it, right?" Without waiting for an answer, he held her above him and thrust upward.

He filled her entirely from this position, and then one hand reclaimed her breasts. Lisa was surprised at how completely she felt within his power, and at the razor-edged pleasure that ran through her.

Steadying herself with both hands on the bed, she shifted tentatively at first and then with growing confidence along the length of him. Her hair fell wildly around her shoulders, and she lowered her head to swing it across his legs.

From underneath, Ryder pushed into her, faster and tighter. It required her full cooperation to hold their position, and, as she braced herself to assist him, Lisa could feel the power flowing between them. They had become partners, united in ecstasy.

His sighs intensified, and then she realized that some of the joyous noises were coming from her. She couldn't stop to analyze her response; it shone bright as the sun.

His rapid thrusting became an unstoppable force. It made the luminescence around Lisa pulsate and expand, and then she *was* part of Ryder, infused with him, dissolving into him.

She wasn't sure when they stopped moving together, or when the fire ebbed into a soft glow. She found herself lying by his side, his arms holding her.

If only this closeness would last forever! But before they could take their relationship to a new stage, she had to reveal why she'd really come here. He had a right to know the truth.

Before she could find a way to begin, Ryder gave her an opening. "We forgot the condom," he said. "Honey, I hope you're not pregnant."

"Would that be so terrible?" she asked.

A stillness came over him. "You want to have a baby?"

"Well, eventually," Lisa said. "Don't you?"

From where she lay with her cheek against his shoulder, she could feel his head shake. "No."

"Never?" He couldn't mean it.

"Never." The hollowness in his tone bordered on anger. "I'm not father material, and I wouldn't be cruel enough to wish myself on some hapless child."

For a moment, Lisa couldn't swallow. He sounded so furious and final. "Maybe you're not ready to be a father yet—"

"I'll never be ready, and you might as well get used to it," Ryder said.

"What if—I mean, we *did* take a chance this weekend," she reminded him.

A muscle jumped in his jaw. "I'd pay child support, of course. But I—well, I'd have to urge you to consider adoption. A child deserves two parents, and I don't have it in me to be one of them."

She knew there must be some old, deep hurt behind his words, because in Lisa's opinion this energetic, tender man would make an ideal father. But he obviously didn't comprehend that. "You might change your mind one of these days."

"Don't count on it," he snapped. "I hope, Lisa, that you would never stoop so low as to try to trap me. I could never forgive a woman who manipulated me like that."

"I would never want to trap you," she said in a small voice.

His grip around her tightened. "I know. There's a sweetness and honesty about you, in spite of this nonsense about where you do or don't come from. I'd like to see more of you. A whole lot more."

"Of course," Lisa responded automatically, but a painful pressure in her chest warned that it couldn't be.

She might be able to defy her parents' choice of a husband, but she couldn't go so far as to marry a man who refused to have children. Even if she *were* willing, the matter was already out of her hands.

In every way, from the moment they met, she had been deceiving Ryder. Even if she didn't turn out to be pregnant, sooner or later she would have to tell him the whole story. He couldn't help but despise her for it.

Tomorrow morning, early, she had to leave. If Ryder proved to be a heavy sleeper, she might even take the coward's way and sneak out, leaving a note.

He would hate her forever, and she deserved it. She also deserved the broken heart she would carry for the rest of her days.

What she didn't deserve was a baby. But Lisa hoped for one, anyway. Not so much for her parents anymore, but because she would cherish being able to keep even that much of Ryder.

HE AWOKE to clear mountain light and an itchy sense that something was amiss. Ryder patted the bed beside him.

Empty. "Lisa?"

He heard no answering voice, no telltale creak of the floor, no running water in the shower.

A wave of disbelief came, so intense that he wanted to turn over and go back to sleep. Maybe when he awoke he would find that this solitude had been a bad dream.

Then he noticed that the clock read 9:17. It was late enough that she might have gotten up earlier and gone out to get a newspaper or some breakfast. Maybe her absence was only temporary.

Ryder sat up, annoyed at his own anxiety. Just because he made love to a woman didn't mean he had a right to keep her on a leash, did it? Besides, she might not have heard him calling if she were in the kitchen.

He rose, winced as his foot met the floor and hobbled on a short tour of the chalet. He called, "Lisa?"

several times and listened with growing agitation to the silence that followed.

She couldn't have left him. Not when, for the first time in his life, he was beginning to care about someone.

On the kitchen table, he saw a sheet of paper marked with feminine handwriting.

Don't, Ryder thought. *Don't do this to me, Lisa.*

He walked to the table and picked it up. The paper released a drift of perfume that mingled with the leftover scent of tomato soup and sent crystal-sharp memories needling into him.

There were only two words written on the paper: "Sorry. Lisa." Just two words. Not enough to tell him where she'd gone and when she'd be back.

Ryder glanced into the wastebasket. Tiny pieces of torn paper littered the bottom. Too tiny to piece together and find out what she had tried to tell him before she gave up and left this stiletto thrust of a farewell.

He crumpled the paper in his hand. Wadded, it took on substance, as if she had left him something, after all.

Sure, she'd left him something: a deep, burning rage at being tricked and used. He still didn't know what her game was, and he hoped he wasn't going to find out in some particularly unpleasant manner.

Instinctively Ryder went to check his wallet in the bedroom. He didn't recall leaving it in such an open position, but as far as he could tell, nothing had been taken.

Lisa could have copied a credit card number, but he didn't think she'd had petty thievery in mind. He played and replayed in his mind the whole bizarre episode that had begun on the ski slope, but it didn't fit any pattern that Ryder recognized.

He had no more time to waste on Miss Switzerland, or wherever she really came from. On his way to the coffeepot, Ryder tossed the wadded paper into the trash.

That, he told himself, was the last he would ever see or hear of Lisa Schmidt.

Chapter Seven

Lisa wasn't sure how she managed to drive to Denver, return the car at the airport and fly to New York. She felt unnaturally heavy and wondered that the flooring didn't groan beneath her steps.

The flight was well underway before she allowed herself to think about the man she'd left. And the manner in which she'd left him.

This morning at the chalet, she had tried twice to compose an explanation for Ryder, but it always came out jumbled and, worse, self-justifying. Besides, she knew nothing would soften his anger.

Right before she left, she'd tiptoed into the bedroom to gaze at the man as he slept. She didn't need to memorize the rugged strength of his body or the gentleness in his mouth; they were already engraved on her heart. She just wanted to be near him, one last time.

On impulse, she'd flipped open his wallet and taken one of his business cards. It was silly, since she could get the same information from his Web Page, but having the card made her feel as if she were keeping a little piece of him.

He'd been so adamant about not having children!

Yet wasn't there a chance, if she told him all the facts, that he might change his mind?

Lisa shuddered. She didn't think she could bear to see his look of utter disgust, to watch him turn away. That, she realized, was why she had fled.

I never knew I was such a coward.

It *was* cowardly to leave him this way. Straightening up her seat as they prepared for landing in New York, Lisa took a cold, hard look at herself.

She'd never deliberately used or hurt anyone until now. Since adolescence, she had maintained a balancing act between pacifying her parents and enjoying a pleasant—if circumscribed—world that included friends, books, theater and occasional travel in the company of her mother.

Without giving it much thought, Lisa had assumed she could go on that way indefinitely. When the obnoxious Boris Grissofsky came into the picture, Ryder Kelly had seemed like the perfect solution. Convenient and disposable. A daddy with no questions asked.

She'd never expected wild passion, or love so intense she ached.

Ryder felt the same way she did, Lisa was certain. That made it wrong to run out, wrong to leave him in the dark and wrong to dodge the consequences of her own actions.

He deserved the truth. Then if he chose to kick her out, well, that would be up to him.

A quiver of relief ran through her. Frightened as she was at the prospect of going back, she knew it had to be done.

The plane rumbled as the landing gear lowered.

Once the plane landed, she would have to arrange for a ticket back to Colorado.

But would Ryder still be there? He had no reason to stick around a Colorado ski resort today. By the time she returned to Denver, rented a car and drove to the chalet, he would almost certainly be gone.

She could fly to Los Angeles instead. After all, she had Ryder's office address. What if he weren't going there directly, though? He might have some other assignment.

Frustrated, Lisa forced herself to face the other half of her obligation, to come clean with her parents and break off with Boris. She needed to do that before she was free to confront Ryder and, possibly, consider a future with him.

What if she burned her bridges and he couldn't forgive her? It didn't change anything, Lisa decided. She couldn't go back to living the way she had. She would leave home and get a job on her own.

From this day forward, she would stop drifting and take control of her life. Hadn't she discovered during her stint in the Amsterdam office that she enjoyed business? Well, her father had started from scratch, and so could she.

The plane jolted onto the runway. The engines roared as they reversed, and Lisa felt the sudden deceleration.

The future was rushing to meet her, full of uncertainty and painful reckonings. She almost wished she could go back to the way things used to be, when she was a pampered princess in a castle.

That part of her life had ended the moment she fell in love with Ryder Kelly. That Annalisa Maria Von Schmidt De La Pena was dead.

Long live the new one! she thought, and collected her purse from beneath the seat.

LOTHAIRE HAD BEEN his usual amazingly efficient self. He had procured a limousine-style cab, with enough space for Boris to hide under a tarp in the rear.

As soon as Annalisa got into the cab, it would be Boris's job to leap up and clap an ether-infused cloth over her face. Lothaire would whisk them to a private runway, where a Lear jet waited to carry them to the Caribbean.

Now, sweltering under the canvas and listening to the roar of airplanes landing nearby, Boris had time to consider that this plan might not be as foolproof as he had imagined.

For one thing, he had failed to consider that Lisa might step out of the airport and hail a random cab just as it cruised by. Or that she might walk up to a line of waiting cabs and choose one.

Worse, he was beginning to wonder if he might be setting a trap as much for himself as for Miss De La Pena.

Here he crouched in the dark, at the mercy of Lothaire. Not that Boris suspected his associate of planning to abduct him, but all possibilities had to be considered. He was putting an enormous amount of trust in a man who had only worked for him for a year and a half.

Lothaire, who earned a modest salary and knew the precarious state of Boris's finances, was breaking numerous laws by helping abduct Annalisa. What did the young man expect to gain?

Boris hoped he had no secret agenda. He needed

Lothaire. Hiring the young man had been a rare break in a streak of bad luck going back several years.

It had been bad luck that made several major deals go sour; that, and the dishonesty and incompetence of others. Now Boris owed a hundred thousand dollars to the Yakuza, which paled in comparison to what he'd already lost to the Russian mob.

Soon after Lothaire was hired, the young man had suggested the marriage to Annalisa as a way out. Boris had rejected the idea at first. He was, after all, distantly related to the Hohnersteins, and the girl was nothing but the spoiled child of an upstart Dutch secondhand dealer.

Schuyler Schmidt had added the "von" for effect, and adopted his wife's aristocratic Spanish name after they married. Boris had only come around when it was pointed out that the daughter had noble blood on her mother's side, and that her dowry alone would bail out his debts, while her eventual inheritance should set him up for life.

He hadn't counted on having to sink to such depths to snare her. How infuriating that a brilliant entrepreneur like Boris should be forced to act like a street thug!

He quivered with outrage. How dare this girl humiliate him? After they were married, she would pay the price.

Someone rattled the door handle, so close that Boris jumped. The cab sat at the curb, and now he realized a customer was demanding a ride.

"Out of service!" shouted Lothaire from the front seat.

"Your sign is lit!" a man's voice replied. "Open up!"

"The cab's taken!"

A pounding on the window made the fillings jump in Boris's teeth. "I'm in a hurry! Unlock the damn door!"

"Go away!" From the growl in Lothaire's voice, Boris feared the man might pull a gun. Thank goodness his employee was never hotheaded.

"I'll file a complaint with the authorities! Now let me in!" The man jerked the door so hard the cab rocked.

Boris had had enough. Flinging off the hated tarp, he bared his teeth and leaped toward the window. A little round-faced man jumped back so fast his glasses flew to the sidewalk.

"I told you it was taken!" called Lothaire, and pulled away from the curb.

His blood still racing, Boris couldn't bring himself to hide again. "I feel like an idiot."

"Some things are unavoidable," said Lothaire. "Aha! There she is!"

"Where?" Peering ahead, Boris glimpsed a tall, smartly dressed figure striding along the sidewalk towing a suitcase on wheels. Her long black hair floated in the spring air and her eyes glowed like emeralds. His prize. His treasure.

She was waving for a taxi.

"Get down!" Lothaire rasped.

As he started to duck, Boris glimpsed another cab cutting in front of them. No doubt the driver had also seen this well-heeled target.

A string of exotic curses escaped Lothaire's lips as he jockeyed for position. Frozen by horrified fascination, Boris remained in a squat, staring as the object of his machinations signaled the cab ahead of them and stepped from the curb.

"Get her!" he shouted. "Go!"

Lothaire stomped on the gas pedal. They shot forward so abruptly that Boris fell against the rear seat.

The car bucked and squealed to a halt amid the shattering of glass and the scream of a bystander. Boris flew forward, bounced, and landed on the floor.

The motor died. As Boris slowly raised himself, he saw Lothaire's hands making futile fists against the steering wheel.

"What happened?" gasped Boris.

"We hit her."

"Who?"

"Get out." Lothaire ripped off his seat belt. "Hurry!"

Reaching shakily for his door handle, Boris spotted a cluster of people in the roadway ahead of them. Between their legs, he could see a black-haired woman lying on the ground.

They had hit Annalisa. Rotten luck. But all might not be lost. "Let's scoop her up and get out of here."

"She might be dead." His associate kicked open the driver's door. "And if we don't pull a disappearing act, we might as well be, too."

Dead? Annalisa, his last hope?

Boris would still have voted in favor of snatching her, but Lothaire was elbowing his way through the crowd, headed for a distant taxi stand. He was the only one who knew where to find their chartered plane.

After exiting the cab on the traffic side, Boris sneaked around to the sidewalk. Everyone was too busy fussing over Annalisa or gesturing at the escaping cabbie to notice him.

Desperately, he elbowed his way toward the center of the confusion. Annalisa lay like a rag doll, her suitcase and purse arrayed around her.

Her chest heaved and she stirred. Relief crackled through him. She was alive!

Sirens wailed, and Boris forced himself to head away through the throng as if he had a flight to catch. How seriously she might be injured, and how he would manage to snatch her, remained uncertain.

It didn't matter. Now that he knew she lived, he was going to get Annalisa, one way or another.

THROUGH LAYERS OF MIST she felt a huge throb of pain. It pulsed and skittered, shrank and grew, until at last she pinpointed its location.

My head hurts. She tried to speak the words aloud, but her mouth refused to obey.

She became aware that she was being wheeled on a gurney. The smells of disinfectant and medicine, along with a disembodied voice calling a Dr. Huang to the emergency room, confirmed that she was in a hospital.

They rounded a corner. Every rattle and bump made her head ache.

She wanted someone to hold her hand. Someone specific, except she couldn't put a face to the feeling. Mother? Husband? She didn't know.

The gurney turned again and moved forward more slowly. Angled. Stopped.

"You take her shoulders," said a man's voice. Arms gripped Lisa, and she found herself being jerked through the air, landing on a bed not much softer than the gurney.

"Is she awake?" a man said briskly, from a short distance away.

"Her eyelids are fluttering," responded a woman who must be the nurse. "Officer, she's suffered a serious head injury. I doubt she's in any shape to answer questions."

"We need to talk to her," came the male voice. "As soon as possible."

Someone pulled a sheet over her, but didn't notice she was awake. Maybe that was because she couldn't pry her eyelids apart.

She wanted someone to tell her what was going on. Mostly, she wanted someone at her side who loved her, but she couldn't remember who that might be.

"Has someone notified her next of kin?" asked the nurse.

"That's the problem," said the officer. "She has a Swiss passport in the name of Lisa Schmidt, which we think might be forged. We're checking on it now. She also has an international driver's license in the same name, and about two thousand dollars. Plus a plane ticket to Paris, paid for in cash."

"You think she's involved in some kind of illegal activity?" the nurse asked.

No, she wanted to say. *I wouldn't do anything like that.*

"It's possible. Here's the really strange part," said the policeman. "The cab that struck her had a phony license. The driver fled before we got there."

"He hit her on purpose?" asked the nurse.

"That's why we need to talk to her," said the policeman. ''To find out who she is and whether we've got a hit-and-run or an attempted homicide.''

She tried to speak, to let them know she was awake, but darkness whirled around her. Just before she lost consciousness, she realized something that made no sense.

She didn't know why she had false papers, and the name Lisa Schmidt didn't ring any bells. She didn't even know what her name was!

She remembered nothing, nothing at all.

THE LADY WHO OWNED the takeout Chinese restaurant next to Ryder's office was painting out the overnight graffiti from an exterior wall as he drove up. On the far side, the pawnshop manager was rolling up his protective grill for the day.

Ryder parked his car between two buckled piles of asphalt and exited. The mingled smells of fresh paint and exhaust fumes made him grimace. For one disgusted moment, he wished he had stayed in the mountains of Colorado.

It wasn't so much the fresh air he missed, though. In spite of a well-cultivated ability to put disappointments behind him, Ryder couldn't stop thinking about the woman he'd lost.

She had haunted him on the plane ride to L.A. and slept with him in his dreams last night. He'd awakened almost certain that he could hear her breathing.

Walking toward his office had brought Ryder back to reality. A reality of cracked pavement and gutters full of gum and candy-bar wrappers.

The Chinese lady smiled at him. ''It is good to see you. I feel safer when you are here.''

''Him?'' grunted the pawnshop dealer, his ponytail

twitching indignantly. "He don't even carry a gun. You ever see what I got behind my counter?"

"A detective has a stronger image," sniffed the woman. "The bad guys are afraid of him."

"That's because they're stupid," grumbled the shopkeeper, and went inside.

Ryder chuckled. He knew the value of projecting the right image, all right. That was why he kept his hair short and wore a dark suit.

That was also why, three years ago, he'd taken out a five-year lease on an office in this shabby minimall west of downtown. For the same money, he could have rented a larger place in any of a dozen nicer communities. But, rinky-dink as it might be, this strip had a Los Angeles address.

That meant something to the people all over the world who read his Web Page. Los Angeles. Instant recognition that conjured up images of Humphrey Bogart.

The bars on his window were getting dusty, he noted as he reached the front. The sign, Ryder Kelly Investigations, needed retouching, too. It was a good thing clients rarely came here in the age of e-mail, faxes and direct international dialing.

He unlocked the door. It was never left open unless he himself was on the premises.

Raccoon-circled eyes brightened as he entered in a jangle of bells. He was glad to see his secretary wasn't out on an audition today.

Since it was hard to find secretaries in Los Angeles and even harder to keep one, Ryder tolerated Zizi's absences. Luckily, she lacked acting talent, so he was in little danger of losing her permanently to the silver screen.

"Hi!" She was wearing her cropped hair red this week, he noticed. Not auburn or strawberry, but the fiery shade of a painful sunburn. "How's the ankle?"

"Better." He sidled through the outer office, between two filing cabinets, a table holding a fax-copier-printer, and Zizi's desk. The air in here had its own special odor: one part cheap perfume, one part fingernail polish and one part dust. "Anything new since I called yesterday?"

"A man named Anthony Callas wants to talk to you pronto!" she chirped. "He left three phone numbers." She handed Ryder a smudged note.

He recognized the name. In a town as trendy as L.A. it paid to keep up with the entertainment trade papers. Anthony Callas produced records and was looking to buy a radio station.

"Did he say what he wanted?"

"It's confidential." Zizi inspected her nails and frowned. "How come they can put a robot on Mars and they can't make polish that doesn't chip? Oh, did that woman get hold of you?"

Ryder felt his hands go cold. Was it possible Lisa had changed her mind? "A woman called? Today?"

"No, last Thursday. I meant to mention it, but I forgot."

He cursed himself for a fool. Of course she wouldn't regret leaving him, now or ever. "Was it Nina McNally? I haven't heard from anyone else."

Zizi wrinkled her nose. "Not her. This woman said she was from, uh, I think she said International Substrate Inc. She saw your ad on the Internet. Her company needed you to find someone in a hurry, she wouldn't say who. She insisted on knowing where you were."

"You told her?" He couldn't keep the sharpness from his tone.

"Was there something wrong with that?"

"Zizi, my whereabouts are not supposed to be public knowledge." Ryder didn't want to come down on her too hard, though, for fear she might quit. So far, Zizi had been here eight months; his previous three secretaries had lasted five weeks, three months and one week, respectively.

"She made it sound so crucial!" Zizi said. "I, uh, guess I talk too much, huh?"

Ryder bit back a cutting retort. "In future, please don't give out my location." Then the oddity of the situation struck him. A woman claiming to represent an international firm had learned his whereabouts but hadn't called him at the chalet. A short time later, Lisa turned up on the slope.

Was it possible their encounter hadn't been a co-incidence? "Did this woman have a foreign accent?"

Zizi shook her head. "Only if you count saying 'eh' twice, the way Canadians do."

A Canadian? Definitely not Lisa. "She never reached me. I guess they found someone else for the job."

Ryder went into his office and punched in the office number for Anthony Callas. On the first ring a man answered. "Callas here."

"Ryder Kelly. You wanted to talk to me?"

"How good are you at finding runaways?" The producer's voice bristled with tension. "My daughter is gone."

"You're sure she ran away of her own free will?"

"She left a note," Callas said. "I don't want the

police involved. I just want to make sure she's all right.''

''I have a good track record with runaways,'' Ryder said. ''Usually, they don't go far.''

''Ginger's sixteen and she'll trust anybody except the one person who really cares about her.'' The man sounded as if he was angry and hurting at the same time.

They agreed on a retainer and set a meeting for that afternoon at Callas's home in Beverly Hills. Ryder hung up, hoping he could help the man and prevent the girl from harm.

The new case, and some other loose ends he needed to clear up, ought to keep him busy for a while. If he were lucky, they would also keep thoughts of Lisa Schmidt at bay until time and distance banished her permanently from his dreams.

LISA AWOKE EARLY. She could hear people moving through the hospital corridor, but the bed next to hers lay empty. There was no sign of the policeman.

Her body felt bruised but her mind prickled, as if warning that she shouldn't be lying here. Someone might have tried to kill her, wasn't that what the officer had said?

He'd questioned her briefly the previous night. She wasn't sure he'd believed that she had amnesia, but the nurse had come to her rescue when he tried to press her.

He'd seemed more concerned about her forged papers than about her safety. But if someone had tried to kill her once, it might happen again.

Who would want to hurt her, and why? Until she recovered her memory, Lisa, or whatever her real name was, had no way of knowing, but a rising restlessness refused to let her doze.

Stiffly, she sat up and swung her legs over the edge of the bed. Her head swam and her stomach twisted, and she sat motionless until her equilibrium returned.

From beneath a bandage on her arm, a tube connected her to a hanging container of clear fluid. Even though she couldn't remember her own name, somehow she knew that it contained nutrients and medicine.

She needed to keep her mind clear, not fogged with painkillers.

With slow, deliberate movements, Lisa opened a drawer in the bedside table and found a wad of cotton and a Band-Aid. With skill that came from some obscure, intact corner of her mind, she unwrapped her arm, pulled out the needle at the end of the tube, and stopped the blood with pressure from the cotton ball.

After applying the Band-Aid, she pushed the intravenous tube away. Sluggishly she got to her feet, and had to press one hand against the edge of the bed to offset the dizziness.

A small door led into a bathroom. Pulling the skimpy hospital gown around her, Lisa shuffled toward it.

Inside, she flicked on a light and turned to wash her face. That was when she saw the woman in the mirror.

A white bandage sat on the side of her head like a misshapen cloche hat. From beneath it, long black hair straggled limply.

The face had to be hers, but it belonged to a stranger. Panic surged through Lisa. *I don't even rec-*

ognize myself. How can I know who to trust? Where can I go?

Gripping the edge of the sink, she struggled to reassure herself. Amnesia following a head injury would surely pass. In the meantime, it was no wonder she failed to recognize a face so purple with bruises.

Lisa washed as best she could. Her body urged her to return to bed, but her mind rebelled.

She vaguely remembered making a decision not to drift, not to leave her fate in the hands of others.

When had she made such a vow? Under what circumstances?

Lisa eased out of the bathroom and surveyed the room. The main door to the corridor stood slightly ajar. To her right a smaller door indicated a closet. With any luck it held her possessions.

Inside she found a dark blue suitcase and a gray purse. They must be hers, although she didn't recognize them.

With trembling hands she opened the pocketbook and poked through its contents. The small silver comb and brush showed exquisite workmanship. So did the metallic makeup kit and the small vial of perfume. She knew that scent, though, or some part of her did; it gave her a buoyant sense of well-being when she dabbed some on her throat.

Lisa found a plane ticket, but no passport. According to the policeman, she was supposed to be Swiss, yet her flight terminated in Paris. Had she been expecting someone to meet her there?

The wallet, to her disappointment, contained no photographs. However, the international driver's license was still there, along with more than two thousand dollars in cash.

Lisa fingered the wad of bills. She was grateful that the authorities hadn't held her belongings, even though they probably should have.

Her fingers bumped a stiff paper edge, and she pulled a business card from where it lay half-hidden in the bill compartment.

"Ryder Kelly Investigations. We specialize in missing persons." It gave a Los Angeles address and phone number. Since the officer hadn't asked her about the card, apparently he hadn't noticed it.

She turned it over, but there was nothing written on the back. Still, in the absence of any other information, the card might be significant.

Had she been trying to find a missing person? Had she contacted this investigator? If so, he might hold a precious clue to her past.

Paris or Los Angeles? Where should she go?

In the hallway, footsteps squeaked. Shoving the items back into the closet, Lisa stumbled with as much speed as possible into the bathroom.

"Hello?" came a nurse's voice. "Are you all right?"

"I'm in here," Lisa called. "I'll be out in a few minutes." *Please don't let her notice I've disconnected the IV.*

After a pause, the woman said, "I'll come back, then."

Rubber-soled shoes squeaked away. As Lisa emerged, she saw that the main door stood open wider than before, but not far enough for passersby to see much of the room.

Outside, carts rattled and voices spoke in crisp tones. It was a typical morning in the hospital, she thought, and wondered how she could remember such mundane details when important facts had deserted her.

After retrieving clothes from the suitcase, Lisa changed in the bathroom. She chose dark slacks and a multicolored sweater, and a ski cap to cover her bandaged head. In the mirror, she applied foundation to minimize the bruises.

The fuzziness in her brain metamorphosed into a pounding headache. Only an overriding sense of urgency kept her moving.

She had to get out of here. Did she dare take the suitcase? It was heavy and might attract attention, but she couldn't bring herself to leave it behind.

Now for the hardest part. She had to sneak out of the hospital and find her way to an airport and catch a flight to…

Paris? It seemed the logical choice. She had the ticket in her purse.

But it was for a flight that had already departed. Besides, once her absence was discovered, the police might be looking for her to try to flee the country. And she had no passport.

If anyone was waiting for her in Paris, he or she would have left the airport by now anyway. The only person whose address she had, the only one she could turn to, was a detective named Ryder Kelly.

She hoped he could help her.

Chapter Eight

She had vanished. Walked out right under the noses of the police and the hospital staff.

Standing in the living room of his fifteen-hundred-dollar-a-night hotel suite, Boris aimed a string of curses at his hapless associate, ending with, "It was your job to prevent this, you cretin!"

Lothaire lit a cigarette off the dying ember of his last one, tossed the butt aside and ground it into the carpet with his heel. "It wasn't easy to learn where they had taken her. By the time I arrived, Miss De La Pena had made her exit."

"How could a woman with a serious head injury walk out of a hospital?" Boris fumed. "Carrying a suitcase!"

"This is New York. Nobody pays attention to anybody else." Nevertheless, Lothaire looked displeased with himself.

At least the young man had turned up again promptly. He could have sneaked away and kept going, especially since his replacement paycheck had also bounced.

"What about our filmmaker friend?" Boris demanded. "Has his girlfriend heard anything from An-nalisa?"

"He doesn't know," Lothaire said.

"Why not?" Boris snapped. "She's either made contact or she hasn't!"

"His girlfriend wouldn't approve of his selling in-formation to us. He has to spy on her."

"He should beat it out of her!"

"Then, obviously, she would leave, and he would learn nothing." Lothaire's upper lip began to curl, but he got it under control. "Did I mention an interesting twist? According to hospital gossip, the mystery woman developed amnesia."

"You mean she doesn't know who she is?"

"That's what people generally mean by 'amne-sia.'" The young man's voice had a caustic note. From tension, no doubt.

"She could be wandering in the street?"

"It took planning to sneak out of there undetected, so I do not believe she is mentally incompetent. Also, she had plenty of cash. Who knows where she might go?"

That was when the brilliant idea came to Boris. It gave him the expansive warmth he felt when he was winning at cards or besting another businessman on a deal. "You are sure she hasn't gone home?"

"Definitely," said Lothaire. "I have contacted the maid. Also, our heiress has made the police suspi-cious by sneaking away, and they have alerted the airlines to watch for her on international flights. If she had taken one, I would know it by now."

"The police have no idea who she is?"

"They do not," confirmed Lothaire.

"And neither does she." Boris couldn't resist an excited quiver.

"Her memory may return at any time," said his aide.

"That is an unknown element, I admit." Boris decided not to worry about it. Nothing ventured, nothing gained. "When she does not return as promised, her parents will be worried." Seeing no response from his associate, he added, "The more time passes, the more frantic they will become."

Lothaire regarded him assessingly. "It could be several days. Even weeks."

"A week should be long enough," said Boris.

"Long enough for what?" It was a pleasure to see his assistant in the dark, for a change.

"Long enough for me to get my hands on a large amount of money immediately, without having to wait for the wedding."

The young man slanted him a look of grudging admiration. "You intend to seek a ransom?"

"When they do not hear from her and they receive my e-mail, it should not be hard for them to believe that she has been kidnapped."

"They might call the police."

Why was his associate finding flaws in his brilliant plan? "We will threaten to kill the girl unless the kidnapping is kept hush-hush. The best part," Boris added with a chuckle, "is that when she turns up safe and sound and Schuyler Schmidt realizes he was conned, he will be too embarrassed to report it."

"You may be right," Lothaire conceded. "He will not want his trading partners to believe he is easily cheated."

Things were looking up, Boris decided as he

opened his laptop and sat down to rough out his e-mail to the De La Penas. He could net a fabulous ransom and still claim Annalisa as his bride after she returned.

All she had to do was to stay lost a little while longer.

RYDER WAS HAVING one of those days that he'd just as soon forget.

First, he was awakened at 3 a.m. by seductive images of Lisa undulating through his brain. Struggling to subdue his rising desire, he focused instead on a burning urge to tell her exactly what he thought of her. Since she wasn't around to vent his wrath on, he lay awake, fuming, for two hours, until he gave up and arose at 5 a.m.

After working out at the gym, he arrived at the office early and spent an hour consulting by phone with a potential client from the East Coast. The man plied him with questions about his techniques, then waffled about engaging his services. Just another lookie-loo in search of free information, Ryder concluded in annoyance.

The morning was spent interviewing Ginger Callas's teenage friends. He received only one solid tip: she liked to hang out at the beach.

In Beachside, to be specific. The resort community had the advantage of being a mere half-dozen miles from Ryder's apartment. On the other hand, this week marked spring vacation, which meant the area would be swarming with kids.

Seaside apartments rented by the week, and youthful tenants often let strays sleep in their living rooms. Finding Ginger during spring break would be like try-

ing to locate one particular grain of sand. Especially
since Ryder knew he looked too much like an au-
thority figure to inspire trust among adolescents.

He couldn't afford to muff this case. Not only was
Anthony Callas paying well, but Ryder had been trying for some time to establish a reputation within the
entertainment industry. It would mean more affluent
clients, more interesting cases and less time wasted
on often-elusive bail jumpers.

After a fast lunch, he returned to the office to discover that Zizi had taken the afternoon off to audition
for a game show. Her note didn't say whether she
was trying out as a contestant or for a job as the host's
assistant.

Grumpily, Ryder put in a call to Biff Connor, a
buddy he knew from the gym. Biff owned a surf shop
in Beachside, and Ryder figured maybe he could pass
out advertising as an excuse to circulate on the beach.

"Sorry, but I have to close up for a few days and
drive to Phoenix," Biff said. "My mom just got out
of the hospital with bronchitis and asked me to come
stay with her. I hate to lose the sales, but I'm alone
here. Of course, if you'd like to run the store, you're
welcome to it."

"I'm not much of a shopkeeper. Besides, I need to
be out on the beach, talking to people." Briefly Ryder
entertained the notion of enlisting Zizi to staff the
register, but there was no telling when she'd get back,
and when she did, he needed her in the office.
"Thanks, anyway. I hope your mom feels better."

"The doctor says she'll be fine," Biff said. "But
she took care of me when I was a kid, so I figure I
can do the same for her."

Bells jangled in the outer office. Ryder came to full

alert, as always when Zizi was absent. Might be a client. A solicitor. Or a drug-crazed robber, although he'd never encountered one so far.

"Gotta go," he said. "Thanks, anyway." Hanging up, he launched himself toward the front room.

A whiff of perfume reached him even before he entered. Subtle, teasing, painfully familiar perfume.

Ryder refused to indulge in fantasies as he moved around a file cabinet to face the newcomer. No doubt a lot of women used that scent. "May I help...?" He stopped.

At first glance the woman standing in front of the desk was obviously Lisa. At second glance he could see marked differences.

The green eyes were unchanged, but they peered from a face grown puffy and discolored. Black hair straggled from beneath a lumpy ski cap, and her shoulders hunched as if in pain.

"Are you Ryder Kelly?" she asked uncertainly.

Ryder narrowed his eyes suspiciously, his jaw tightening with unspoken caustic responses. Martial arts training had taught him that whoever attacked first yielded the advantage, so he waited. But he wondered what her game was.

"Do you know who I am?" she asked.

A quick, impatient breath escaped him. "Why don't you get to the point?"

Her still-beautiful face projected confusion and vulnerability. Incredibly, she could almost convince him, even now, that she hadn't a deceitful bone in her body. "I think my name is Lisa Schmidt but I'm not sure. I found your business card in my wallet, and I was hoping I'd talked to you before."

"We've met," Ryder said coolly.

"We have?" She brightened hopefully. With that acting ability, she should be the one going to auditions, not Zizi. "Then you know my name?"

"You said it was Lisa Schmidt, but you were lying," he growled.

"You don't know who I am?"

"I haven't got a clue. What's more, I don't care."

Lisa sagged against the desk. Ryder didn't want to get drawn into her trickery again, but a gentlemanly instinct made him come around to help her.

When he touched her elbow, he realized she was shaking. As she sank into a chair, he got a disturbing closer look at her injuries.

Beneath the makeup, the entire side of her face had turned black-and-blue. The cap rode up to reveal the edge of a thick bandage that didn't entirely cover a spreading purple bruise.

There was no question that she'd been badly knocked around. "You need a doctor," he said.

"No!" Panic made her rise halfway before dropping back.

"Why not?"

"Someone's trying to kill me," she whispered.

"Probably some old boyfriend," he muttered, and then wished he hadn't spoken the words aloud.

"What do you mean?" Panic yielded to curiosity. "Mr. Kelly, do I know you in other than a professional capacity?"

"Only if you count spending a weekend in bed together." For once, Ryder was glad his secretary had gone out. He would never have dared be so blunt in her presence.

"I slept with you?" Two dark eyebrows arched as she regarded him. Speculation colored her gaze as it traversed his body, from his face to his chest and down to the rebelliously awakening region below.

"I must have made quite an impression," he growled. "To be forgotten so quickly."

"Quickly?" she asked.

"You walked out on me the day before yesterday."

"Where?"

"In Colorado," he said. "Give me a break, Lisa. You can't have forgotten—"

"So *that's* what I was doing at the wrong airport," she said. "I wondered why I was at LaGuardia when my flight left from JFK. I must have just arrived."

"Care to elaborate?" He was glad to see that at least she no longer seemed on the verge of fainting. If she did, he might have to catch her in his arms, an unsettling possibility.

"I had a plane ticket to Paris in my purse, along with a fake Swiss passport," Lisa said. "I don't remember what happened but the officer said a cab hit me and the driver ran off."

"At LaGuardia?" he asked.

"Yes. I woke up in the hospital. The police said the taxi's permit turned out to be fake, like my passport."

"So we have a virtual cornucopia of bogus documents," Ryder grumbled. He wished her story didn't sound so convincing, but she had obviously been injured somehow.

"That's why they think I might have been hit on purpose," Lisa said. "They also suspect I might have been involved in something illegal, but I'm sure I wasn't. It's scary. I can't remember who I am, or anyone I know, including you." She studied him again. "You're *sure* I walked out on you?"

"Yes."

"We spent how long in bed together?"

"Two days," he said.

"You must know something about me," she pressed. "How did we meet? Who introduced us? People don't just jump into—I mean, I don't think I'm the type to—did I?"

"You didn't jump," he said. "You leaped with great abandon."

"That's awful."

"It wasn't that awful."

"I mean, it's awful that I don't remember any of it!"

Darn it, she'd nearly made him laugh. Ryder didn't want to like Lisa, or whatever this woman's name was. He wanted to keep on being mad at her.

Underneath, he knew he was being played for a fool all over again. But her tactics made even less sense now than they had at the chalet.

"Let me see if I'm following this," he said. "You got creamed by a cab and landed in the hospital. The police said you were in danger, so naturally you checked right out—"

"Sneaked out," Lisa said.

"The hospital didn't release you?"

"I'm not even sure they ever admitted me. At least, not properly, since they don't know who I am." She frowned. "I seem to know a few things about hospitals."

"You used to work in one," he said.

"I'm a nurse?"

"Volunteer work. You're a rich girl, or so you said."

She took a moment to digest that idea. "Maybe

you should take me shopping and see if I naturally veer toward the expensive labels.''

That did make him laugh. ''I can't believe you're joking at a time like this.''

''Neither can I.'' Her ironic smile set his sucker of a heart to waltzing. ''I guess this sounds odd, but I've got about fifteen hundred dollars left, and I'll pay you to find out who I am.''

''If you spend all your money on me, what are you going to live on? This could take a while.'' He remembered Zizi's mention of a phone call that might provide a clue. ''Have you ever heard of International Substrate Inc.?''

She stretched her long, slender legs. ''I don't know.''

''Have any friends from Canada?''

''I wish I knew whether I had any friends, period.''

He cast about for other possibilities. ''You said you had a plane ticket to Paris. Do you speak French?''

She frowned. ''I...I don't know....''

''Can you say 'I love you'?''

''*Je t'aime.*''

''How about Spanish?''

''*Te amo.* In German, it's *Ich liebe dich.*'' She said it in two more languages that he didn't recognize but which she claimed were Dutch and Russian.

''Do you actually speak those languages?'' he asked.

''I don't know,'' she admitted. ''Maybe I just like to tell people I love them. Do you want me to try any other phrases?''

''I have a better idea. Keep your money. I can't help you.''

Tears glittered. ''Mr. Kelly—I guess I should call

you Ryder, considering what we've been to each other, shouldn't I?—I'm sorry for the way I behaved. I honestly don't understand it. I don't even know what kind of person I am, or was. But please, you're the only one I can turn to.''

Ryder hadn't risen from poverty through the hard knocks of the Marine Corps and the grinding work of a rookie cop to be wrapped around the finger of a woman who'd already treated him like dirt. On the other hand, what if she really were in danger?

People who traveled with false passports and large amounts of cash generally kept risky company. Maybe she was a courier who'd run afoul of some high-level criminal organization. Maybe she'd fallen for Ryder and had left him for his own good.

Yeah, sure. And pigs could fly.

He couldn't bring himself to throw her out. If she came to harm, he would never forgive himself.

The thought of harm reminded him that he was supposed to be searching for Ginger Callas. Which gave him a useful idea.

"How would you like to spend the rest of the week working at the beach?" he asked.

"YOU PRESS THIS KEY and the register figures the sales tax," said the tattooed man at the counter. "Do you remember everything I've told you?"

"Sure." At least, Lisa hoped she did. There didn't appear to be anything wrong with her memory concerning the present.

"The directions are right under here," said the shop owner, indicating a shelf beneath the front counter. "In case you need a refresher."

"She might not, Biff, but I will," Ryder remarked from where he stood.

"You aren't supposed to be working the register," his friend pointed out. "You're supposed to be bringing in new business."

Lisa followed his gaze out the open doorway of the small shop. The vista of beach and ocean was lovely, if utterly strange to her. On the other hand, she might have lived here all her life and not know it.

"We're going in the back room to design an advertising flyer." Ryder's brown eyes searched her face as if he could see into her soul. "Do you feel okay sitting here by yourself?"

"Sure," she said.

"Not dizzy?"

"Not anymore." He'd insisted that she eat lunch, something Lisa had overlooked, and she felt stronger. It pleased her that she was recovering so quickly from her accident. She didn't want to be a burden. "I hope I won't hurt your business, Biff."

"Are you kidding?" He pushed back a strand of bleached blond hair and regarded her admiringly. "Car accident or not, with a chick like you at the counter, I'll have half the surfers in Beachside coming in to shoot the breeze."

"Shoot the breeze?" She struggled to make sense of the phrase. "Does that mean I'm supposed to give sailing lessons?"

Biff guffawed. "Not hardly."

"It means you're supposed to look pretty and pretend the surfers are saying something intelligent," grumbled Ryder. "Which isn't likely."

"Someone wouldn't be jealous, would he?" Biff asked.

"Why don't you help me put a flyer together and spare me the psychoanalysis?" returned the detective, and led the way to the back.

Alone, Lisa balanced on a stool behind the counter and took her bearings.

Late-afternoon sunshine flowed through the gray-tinted front window and mingled with fluorescent light to soften the Hawaiian colors of swimwear and souvenir towels. Racks of surfboards, skateboards, bodyboards and shiny black wet suits lined the walls.

Toward the center of the shop, tiered shelves offered goods from suntan lotion to goggles. A glass case by the register featured underwater watches, thermometers and other small devices.

The scent of brine hung in the air, and the lazy hum of the ocean was punctuated by seagull cries. On the sidewalk outside, two children stood supporting their bicycles while they licked ice cream cones.

For the first time since she'd awakened at the hospital, Lisa discovered a sense of peace. It might be due to the serenity of her surroundings, but she knew it had something to do with Ryder, too.

Even if he hadn't told her that they knew each other, she would have sensed it. Or perhaps she'd simply known instantly, when he emerged from his inner office, that she *wanted* to know him.

She liked his muscular chest and shoulders, well-developed but not bulky. The way he moved revealed alert self-control, as if he were always poised for action.

His short brown hair seemed in need of rumpling, and his mouth curved endearingly when anything amused him. Instinctively she knew that he needed only to touch her, to hold her, and she would yield to him eagerly.

How frustrating not to remember how it felt to sleep with the man! She couldn't imagine why she would have left him.

Two girls of twelve or thirteen wandered in, barefoot and glistening with suntan oil. They poked along one shelf, examining the lip gloss.

Could one of them be Ginger Callas? They looked too young to fit Ryder's description of the runaway, and neither was a redhead, but perhaps they'd seen her.

"Can I help you?" she asked.

The shorter of the pair glanced up. "Hey, what happened to you? Run into a door?"

"Car accident," Lisa said.

"Don't mind Buffy," said her companion. "Aren't you awfully hot in that sweater?" She herself wore a racing-striped swimsuit with cutouts at the waist.

"All Starr ever thinks about is clothes," explained Buffy, who wore an orange stretch top over a purple bikini bottom.

"I just got into town," Lisa explained. "I'm helping a friend for a few days. My wardrobe's a little on the warm side."

"You oughta try one of those sarongs." Starr indicated a rack of flowered swimsuit coverups.

Buffy scrutinized Lisa again. "What kind of car accident? Were you driving?"

"No, I was walking." Lisa tried to imitate their loose-jawed manner of speech. "In the wrong place at the wrong time, obviously."

That apparently satisfied Buffy, because she moved on to a new topic. "Where are you from? Like, Hawaii or something? Or maybe Italy? You look like you should be named Leilani or maybe Sophia.''

''It's Lisa. And I'm not from anywhere special.''

Starr handed her a camouflage-print hat with a brim. ''You could wear this instead of that knit thing.''

''Thanks, but I'm afraid it would clash with a sarong.'' Lisa decided that she *could* afford to buy a few new clothes, since Ryder had offered her a place to stay rent-free. ''By the way, I'm supposed to meet a girl named Ginger, but I can't find her. She has curly reddish blond hair, and her favorite T-shirt shows Brad Pitt on the front. Have you seen her?''

''If we do, we'll let you know.'' Starr stopped in dismay as Ryder emerged from the back room. ''Who's *that?*''

''Oh, he's doing some promotional work for the store,'' Lisa said.

''He looks like a cop.'' Her companion backed toward the door.

''See ya,'' said Starr.

Ryder watched them go. ''I seem to have that effect on people around here. Learn anything useful?''

''That I need new clothes.''

''Twenty-percent discount,'' Biff said as he emerged behind Ryder.

Eyeing the rack, Lisa decided to heed the girls' suggestion. Tomorrow, she would pick out a wrap-around dress, even though it would bare her bruised shoulder. At least the flowered pattern might draw attention away from her injuries, and it would be a lot cooler than what she was wearing. ''I gave them Ginger's description. They said they'd watch for her.''

Ryder regarded her ruefully. "You got through to them without even trying. One glance at me and they couldn't get out of here fast enough."

"That's because you look like a narc." Biff tossed him a package of stick-on tattoos. "Try some of these. There's a shop down the block where you can get ragged cutoffs and baggy T-shirts."

"Then will I fit in?" Ryder asked dubiously.

"No. But at least you'll look like a narc who's trying to be one of the crowd," said his friend.

"Thanks a bunch." Tugging his suit jacket into place, Ryder helped Lisa down from the stool. "We'll be back in the morning."

Biff gave him a spare key and the combination to the security alarm. "Here's the phone number at my mother's, if you have any questions."

"We'll be sure to call," said Lisa.

"I'm sure we'll be fine on our own," Ryder said at the same time.

"You, my friend, can be fine on your own, and Lisa can call me," Biff said. "Anytime." He winked, then ducked playfully as if dodging a blow.

Outside, Lisa asked, "Was he flirting with me?"

"You might say that." Ryder squinted at the throng of bodies spread across the sand.

"Why?" Lisa asked. "I'm a mess."

Ryder sidestepped a stroller. He favored his right leg slightly, as if it were sore. "Yes, but you're a gorgeous mess."

"Thank you." In view of the way she'd apparently mistreated him, she was surprised he would compliment her. In any case, she didn't feel beautiful. She felt battered and sore and, all of a sudden, tired. "Would you mind if I took a nap?"

Ryder glanced at his watch. "It's after five. Time to head home."

They passed a sign announcing Fortunes Told Here. A white-haired man in a toga stood in front, eyes half-shut, chanting a mantra.

"What's he doing?"

"Acting normal, for him, I would guess," Ryder said. "The beach is a natural refuge for weirdos."

"Why would he wear a toga?"

"How come you know it's a toga when you don't know your own name?"

"I remember a lot of things," she explained as they reached the parking lot. "That sarongs come from Pacific islands and togas from Rome. But not where I come from."

"It's hard for me to believe this isn't a trick." Ryder unlocked his blue sedan, reached in and removed a sunshade that had covered the windshield. "About losing your memory."

"I'm not sure I want it back," she admitted. "You make it sound as if I wasn't a very nice person."

"You weren't very nice to me." He opened the passenger door and held it for her. "I can't say how you treated other people."

"Apparently I made somebody want to kill me," she said, and got in.

Ryder glanced around uneasily. "Lisa, I can't guarantee your safety, especially not while I'm out looking for Ginger."

She stared at him through the open door. "I feel safe with you, Ryder. Just being near you."

His troubled expression told her that he hadn't forgiven her earlier actions, yet his behavior toward her today had been protective. Now he was taking her to his apartment, where he'd offered the use of a couch.

Lisa wasn't sure how safe she would be from him there. She wasn't sure she wanted to be safe from him at all.

.

Chapter Nine

I am, Ryder thought, the greatest fool who ever walked the earth.

Lisa had dozed off in an easy chair while he broiled pieces of chicken and fixed rice pilaf and a salad. Now, beneath his gaze, she lay sleeping peacefully, dark lashes trembling against her cheek.

Her presence in his apartment changed its dimensions, its atmosphere, even the way the light fell through the blinds. The dark hair fanning around her face and the colorful ski sweater contrasted vividly with the impersonality of his white walls and tan furnishings.

He'd chosen this airy unit in a modern, Spanish-style complex as a bulwark against childhood memories. Outside, maintenance men kept everything sparkling. Inside, neither moldering laundry nor messy little fingerprints bespoiled the pristine surfaces.

Into this sterile setting he had brought an untamed creature who had already demonstrated her power to disrupt his self-control. At this very moment, when he ought to be poking her awake before dinner got cold, he could only stand there looking at her.

He couldn't help being glad that Lisa had turned up today. He didn't even care that she was probably using him again, and that in a few days she would no doubt vanish.

Ryder wanted those days. He craved every hour, every minute. Maybe it was the risk taker in him that found her so fascinating, he admitted. Her very unpredictability added to her charm.

At least he didn't have to worry about her tying him down, he reminded himself ruefully. *Be careful what you wish for: you might get it.* He'd never understood that old saying until now.

Lisa's eyes fluttered open. Ryder watched her intently. In this unguarded moment, she might let slip some clue to her true state of mind.

When she saw him, her mouth curved in unrestrained pleasure. There was no visible effort to bring herself under control, nothing to indicate she might be feigning.

Confusion replaced her lazy good cheer. "I expected—"

"What?"

"A different room."

"Describe it."

"Blue," she said. "And white."

"The chalet." Naturally she would associate him with the place where they'd spent time together. "Your memory is coming back."

"I hope so. Or at least, I think I do." She started to finger comb her hair, then stopped as her hand encountered the bandage. "Ouch."

"Do you remember getting hurt?"

"Not the accident itself. I can recall everything since I woke up at the hospital, though."

It wasn't unusual for a trauma victim to permanently block out the crime or accident itself. As for the rest of her memory, it should return soon enough. "Dinner's ready."

"Good, because I'm starved."

They ate at the small butcher-block kitchen table. As she'd done in the chalet, Lisa kept her fork in her left hand and the knife in her right. The European-style of dining hadn't been a pretense.

Unless, of course, she was still pretending.

"Ryder," she said as she finished a bite of salad. "You refused to take my money, but will you still help me find out who I am?"

"I've already been considering how to proceed," he admitted. "Under normal circumstances, I would circulate your description on the Internet. But if someone might be trying to kill you, we don't want to give them any clues to where you are."

Lisa studied the patterns of rice on her plate as if they were tea leaves. "You really think I'm in danger?"

"We have to go on that assumption," Ryder said, "although the fact that the cab had false papers doesn't necessarily mean it hit you on purpose. What about at the hospital, Lisa? Did you see anyone suspicious?"

Her forehead puckered in concentration. "I don't think so."

"No one tried to stop you on the way out?"

"I pasted a haughty expression on my face and no one dared." Lisa set down her fork. "You know, maybe there's some information in my suitcase that I missed, the way the police overlooked your business card in my wallet. Could we go through it together?"

"It's worth a try."

He washed the dishes and she dried, somewhat clumsily. Ryder wasn't sure whether that was due to inexperience or to her injury.

Finally he realized she was flinching every time she moved her shoulder. "Let's take a look at that."

"It felt stiff earlier. Now it's getting sore." She didn't object as he eased the sweater down.

What he saw made Ryder swear at himself under his breath. The whole side of her body, as far as he could see, had turned an agonizing shade of black and blue.

It should have occurred to him that getting knocked over by a cab would cause serious injuries. How had she managed to get through the day without painkillers?

"You need medicine," he said.

"I don't want my mind fogged up." Lisa slid the sweater into place. "I've got enough memory gaps as it is."

"I'm amazed you can walk around," he said.

"It seems to me..." She pressed her lips together for a moment before resuming. "It seems to me that my own personal feelings aren't very important. That I disregard them. Does that tell you anything about my background?"

"Unfortunately, a lot of people aren't in touch with their feelings," Ryder said. "I don't suppose I am, either. It's not something I spend a lot of time worrying about."

She chuckled. "No time wasted on introspection, eh?"

The "eh" stopped him. Just as Zizi had said, it

sounded Canadian. And Lisa *did* know some French. "Quebec?" he asked. "Is that where you're from?"

"Excuse me?"

"Quebec. In Canada."

"It doesn't ring a bell," she said. "Anyway, I wouldn't need a fake passport or a plane ticket to France if I came from Canada, would I?"

"Presumably not," he agreed, disappointed. "Let me get you some aspirin and then let's go through your luggage."

Still, her use of "eh" strengthened the link between her and the mysterious caller last Thursday. It might have been Lisa herself on the phone, or a Canadian friend whose verbal habit she'd picked up.

Another woman had hunted him down for Lisa? That possibility posed yet another puzzle.

A few minutes later they were sitting in the bedroom with Lisa's clothes and other possessions strewn across the beige comforter. Her light floral scent filled the room.

There was no sign of the tomato-stained clothes. He supposed she had discarded them at her hotel. Wasn't that what a rich girl would do?

Although twilight had arrived, warm light from a lamp bathed the room. "This is a funny bed." From her perch on the padded edge, Lisa pressed the rippling surface.

"Water bed." Ryder felt along the insides of the suitcase. The lining had come loose in a couple of places, so he assumed the police had already searched for secret compartments. He didn't find one.

"Isn't it difficult to go to sleep with the water rippling?" Lisa asked.

"It's quite comfortable." Ryder had bought the

water bed because it was cheap, but he'd been surprised at how well it supported his body. "Does anything here stir any impressions?"

Lisa glanced through a makeup kit, then examined the slacks, blouses, sweaters, and a silky black dress. Ryder tried not to stare at the lacy bras and panties. "They're good quality." She checked a label. "Does this manufacturer's name mean anything to you?"

It didn't. However, when Ryder followed her example, he found that the manufacturers were located in such cities as Paris, Amsterdam, London and Madrid. "You get around."

She stroked a negligee made of cloud-soft aqua silk shot with pink. "Everything here is expensive. You're right—I must be rich."

"In a hurry to get back to it?"

"Not really." She held up a tan scarf through which curved a design reminiscent of a peacock feather. "This might come in handy to cover my bandage."

Ryder's fingertips brushed a satiny rose blouse, until he snatched his hand away. He couldn't help picturing Lisa wearing these garments, and how he would like to remove them, one by one.

An image slammed into his mind of the bathroom at the chalet. Steaming water. A fluffy rug. Lisa, slick, writhing and eager for him.

His body tightened. He yearned to pulled her down on top of him and claim her mouth and breasts and hips until she cried out to be taken.

What stopped him was the realization that she didn't recall making love to him before. How bizarre that, in her heart, he was no longer her lover but a stranger.

"Wouldn't you think I'd have brought something other than clothes and toiletries?" Lisa fiddled with a natural-bristle hairbrush. "There's no diary, no books, no addresses to send postcards to. Either someone took them, or I was deliberately hiding my identity."

"Or both," Ryder pointed out.

Her gaze sobered. "I can't imagine what I was involved in. It's scary. I wish I could just—not go back. Start over as Lisa Schmidt."

So did he. He wanted this fantasy woman to stay. Hard reality would intrude sooner or later, but he was in no hurry for it.

She stifled a yawn. "You take the bed," he said. "I'll be okay on the couch." The couch was too small for him, but he couldn't bear to picture those black-and-blue marks subjected to such discomfort.

"No," she said. "That's too much to ask."

"I'd rather be in the front room, anyway," Ryder said. "To keep watch."

"You think someone followed me to L.A.?"

He didn't, actually. If someone had been tailing Lisa without Ryder noticing him, the guy was either darn good or incredibly lucky.

"I prefer to be cautious." He decided not to help as she began folding her clothes. Touching her private garments would only intensify his urge to touch her instead.

"I don't know what I'd do without you." Large, dark eyes glistened with gratitude.

"Don't worry about it," he said, and got out of there while he could still keep his hands to himself.

In the living room, Ryder stood by the window and surveyed the landscaped grounds of the apartment complex. Illuminated from below, the swimming pool silhouetted the dark figures of tenants swimming and floating on inflatable rafts. Laughter drifted up to him.

Malibu lights marked meandering beds of calla lilies and birds-of-paradise. He saw no questionable movements on any walkways or in the deeper shadows alongside the squatty palm trees.

Of course, a professional surveillance team would rent or sneak into a vacant unit, not lurk in the bushes. Ryder shrugged. His instincts told him that if anyone had followed Lisa when she left the hospital, she would have been grabbed by now.

Flopping onto the couch, he clicked on the TV. One of L.A.'s newscasts droned on, with no word of New York police seeking a missing woman or anything else that might concern Lisa.

She could work at the beach without fear of recognition. Whatever harm she'd caused him—hurt pride if nothing else—Lisa was about to atone for it by helping him find Ginger Callas.

All he had to do was keep his libido in check, survive a few nights on this miserable couch and wait for her memories to return. Then she would go home.

I MUST HAVE left him for his own good.

That was the thought in Lisa's mind when she awoke. Ryder's distinctly male scent had cocooned her all night as she floated on his bed, and she knew she must have been dreaming about him. But if she'd seen anything of the past, it had fled the moment she opened her eyes.

The one certainty that remained was that she had not intended to harm him. That kind of cruelty was not in her nature.

Nor would she have left out of indifference. He wasn't the kind of man a woman would choose to leave. That much had become clear the previous evening.

She'd been intensely aware of him at every moment. Not only of his rough-hewn features and muscular body, but of a subliminal presence that made her skin tingle. Reserved and taut, he radiated mystery, the kind that would keep her awake every night until she solved it.

So, Lisa mused, as she selected some casual clothes and went to shower, she must have left in order to protect him. Which meant that, as soon as she remembered what was going on, she would have to leave again.

She hoped her memory didn't return too quickly. Even though she couldn't recall what her life had been like before, these hours and days with Ryder were special, and always would be.

As they breakfasted, she felt grateful for the distance he kept between them. The way he didn't let their hands touch when he gave her a plate of toast; the way he stared at the newspaper instead of meeting her eyes.

It's for his own good. And mine.

Ryder had dressed in a navy polo shirt and worn jeans. The clothes emphasized the hardness of his body, and Lisa wondered how she had ever found the nerve to make love to such a self-possessed man.

As they descended from the apartment on an outdoor staircase, he refrained from taking her arm. He limped a little, she noticed, and her own muscles felt decidedly stiff. The two of them must look like the walking wounded.

"How did you hurt your leg?" she asked.

He glanced at her in surprise. "Skiing. That was how we met."

"You ran into me?"

"No, I hit someone else. You came over pretending to be a nurse and took my medical history. Then you drove me home and seduced me." Ryder led the way between two buildings to the encircling parking area.

The scenario didn't sound familiar. Lisa tried to push aside the mist in her brain, but that made her head throb. "I'm not a nurse, though."

"You're not from Mee-ami, either," he said.

He must be teasing about something she'd said in her former life. She wished she got the joke.

They drove down a broad avenue lined with car lots, gas stations, minimalls and drive-through restaurants. Lisa didn't see any pedestrians; the entire area was designed for cars, as if they were the dominant life form.

"Tell me more about this girl we're trying to find," she said.

"Ginger Callas? She's sixteen. Her father's a record producer who's made a lot of money."

"What about her mother?"

"Divorced, remarried, divorced again. Not very involved with her daughter." From his shirt pocket, he handed over a color photograph. Lisa studied it.

Red, curly hair. An open, freckled face. Only a slight fullness in the lower lip hinted at adolescent petulance.

It struck her that she and this girl had wealthy backgrounds in common and the fact that they'd both disappeared. How ironic it would be if someone were searching for her, just as she was seeking Ginger.

"You think she's hanging out with friends?"

"I hope so. Anywhere you find unsupervised kids, like the beach, you also find men who prey on them." His words chilled her. "Ginger is naive and headstrong. It's only a question of time before she runs across somebody who could hurt her. We've got to find her first."

"What should I do if I see her?" Lisa asked. "Have her arrested?"

Ryder shook his head. "She hasn't broken any laws. Unless she's in imminent danger, we need to learn where she's staying and notify her father. It's his job to talk her into going home."

"How long do we keep at it? I mean, if she doesn't turn up?"

"You'll be running the store through Sunday. I'll spend part of the time on the beach, but I may have to leave to take care of other business," he said. "Speaking of which..."

On the cellular phone, which fit into a hands-free station in the car, he pressed a rapid-dial button and hit Send. Over the speaker clipped to his car's visor, Lisa heard it ring several times.

A woman's voice answered, "Ryder Investigations."

"It's me." He informed his secretary of their plans for the day. "Page me if anything comes up."

"Will do."

"Oh, Zizi? Any luck with the game show?"

"No, but one of the other contestants is a script reader," she said. "We're going out Saturday night."

"Good luck." As he ended the transmission, Ryder began to chuckle.

"What's so funny?"

"Zizi isn't a writer, so she's wasting her time dating a script reader," Ryder said. "Sometimes she gets carried away with this ambition thing."

"Maybe she's going out with him because she likes him." They must have been nearing the beach, because, through her open window, Lisa could smell salt in the air.

"You're always looking for the best in people," Ryder said. "Maybe you're actually Mary Poppins, except I didn't see you fly in with an umbrella."

"Pollyanna was the one who saw good in everybody, not Mary Poppins," she corrected, and wondered how she could recall the names of literary characters but not her own. The data must, she supposed, be stored in a different part of the brain.

The beach lot lay nearly empty at this hour. A trace of morning fog kept the air cool, and, beyond the asphalt, a watermark on the sand etched the reach of the high tide.

At the surf shop, Ryder unlocked the door and punched in the security code. Lisa felt like an intruder, stepping into the dark store amid the scents of wax and rubber.

The lights came on, banishing the eeriness. "Would you help me review what I'm supposed to do with the cash register?" she asked.

"Have you forgotten already?"

Startled, she realized that Ryder had mistaken her uncertainty for a faulty memory. "No, my brain's functioning fine. I'm intimidated about running this place while you're out on the beach, that's all."

"I'll stay here and help for a while," he assured her. "First, let's see if Biff got the flyers run off."

Everything was ready, and the proper procedures

came to Lisa without a struggle. By the time the first few customers had wandered in and out, with only one making a purchase, she found her confidence growing. She still wasn't qualified to help someone select a surfboard, but then, neither was Ryder.

"If they need assistance, they'll have to wait till Monday," he reminded her about eleven o'clock as he prepared to go and distribute Biff's advertising.

Lisa smoothed down the sarong-style dress that she'd purchased along with a pair of sandals. Judging by Ryder's sidelong glances, the garment flattered her figure.

"You're not going to take his advice and get cut-offs?" she asked.

He shrugged. "Jeans are good enough. Nobody's going to mistake me for a teenager, anyway."

"You don't exactly look like somebody who would be handing out ads for a surf shop." Lisa couldn't resist brushing away a bit of lint from his dark blue shirt. "Maybe you should circulate flyers with Ginger's picture on them instead."

His jaw twitched as her fingers brushed his chest, but he gave no other response. "That would guarantee her going deeper into hiding. Maybe out of the area entirely."

"Good luck, then," she said.

For the next hour, Lisa made idle conversation with customers and rang up a couple of sales. Quite a few young men wandered in for no apparent purpose other than to steal glances at her, which struck her as odd, given her obvious contusions.

When no one was around, she slipped into the changing booth and studied her image in the mirror. She'd removed the bandage this morning before showering, and wrapped the scarf around her head. It made her eyes appear larger than usual, she realized.

Her bruises, which were turning brownish-yellow, faded mercifully beneath the foundation she'd applied. What the men were gaping at, she decided, must be the wraparound dress, which brought out her olive skin tones and bared the upper swell of her breasts.

Was she having the same effect on Ryder? Irrationally, she hoped so. Because every time he came near, a wave of longing shimmered through her.

It was no wonder she'd seduced him in her previous life.

The prospect of putting her arms around Ryder and letting his strong hands stroke her body was almost too delicious to resist.

Tearing herself away from her thoughts, she went out of the booth to watch for customers. Or Ryder. Surely he'd be coming back soon.

It was nearly one o'clock, and Lisa's stomach began to rumble. She'd forgotten to ask about the eating arrangements.

A mother and two children strolled past on the walkway, eating hot dogs. The scent of charcoal grilling drifted inside, and suddenly Lisa wasn't just hungry, she was ravenous.

Reaching under the counter, she retrieved her purse. Most of her money remained at Ryder's apartment, but she'd brought enough to pay for her new clothes, and there were a few dollars left.

Feeling guilty about leaving her post, she hung up a "Be Right Back" sign, closed the door and stepped outside. Two skateboarders clattered by, barely missing her. As she dodged, she squinted against the glare of sunlight no longer softened by the shop's tinted glass.

From inside, she'd caught only occasional glimpses of beachgoers through the window display. Now color and movement flooded her vision: striped umbrellas shading picnickers, beachballs flying and children of all sizes splashing in the surf.

As far as she could see in either direction, hundreds of bronzed bodies roasted on rainbow towels. No wonder it was taking Ryder so long to distribute his flyers. How could he hope to find one girl in this madhouse?

The scent of grilling wafted by again. It emanated, she saw, from a takeout joint two storefronts away, where several bikini-clad young women were lined up at the counter.

How artless and perfect they looked, these California girls with their unmarred tans and minuscule swimsuits. Damp, tangled hair and oversize sunglasses made it impossible to assess their individual characteristics, but Lisa couldn't suppress a twinge of jealousy.

Ryder was spending the day surrounded by nearly naked women. Heck, he lived half a dozen miles away. Once Lisa departed, he would hardly lack for romantic opportunities.

Glumly she went to get in line. The girls ahead of her carted their food away, and she ordered a burger, fries and a soft drink. Not exactly health food, but the desperate would eat anything.

No one appeared interested in the surf shop, and, once she had her lunch sack in hand, Lisa decided she didn't want to risk spilling any food inside. Instead, she passed the store and headed for a nearby bench.

A few steps later she halted abruptly. Outside a curio boutique, a window box overflowed with deep green foliage and vivid red geraniums.

Another image superimposed itself. *Flowers outside my window. Red and yellow tulips.* A memory!

If she stared hard enough at the picture in her mind, Lisa knew she could see more. Maybe the view through the window. A city? A town?

"Hey, uh, Lisa?" A shaggy young man peered at her handwritten name tag. "You work in the surf shop?"

"Yes?" She snapped back to the present. "Did you want to buy something?"

"Not exactly." Long scraggly hair framed the fellow's young, rather sweet face. "This girl, uh, Buffy, said I should check you out because you're a real babe."

Buffy had been the girl on the previous day who wore an orange top and purple bottom, Lisa recalled. "She's matchmaking for me?"

"Not with him!" A shorter fellow, also about eighteen, thrust himself in front of his shaggy companion. Thin-faced and remarkably pale for the vicinity, he had the nervous habit of rubbing his hands together. "I'm more your type, wouldn't you say?"

"No comment." Lisa didn't want to hurt his feelings, but she didn't want to flirt, either. Besides, hunger pangs were making her weak.

Although it was impolite to eat in front of others without offering them any, Lisa couldn't resist nibbling on a couple of French fries. The two young men watched in fascination as she chewed and swallowed.

She hoped Buffy wasn't going to send her any more admirers. Lisa hated being treated like a public spectacle.

Then it occurred to her they might be useful. "Did she tell you I'm looking for a friend of mine named Ginger?"

"Yeah, and that's sort of why—" The first fellow broke off and thrust out his hand. "My name's Jason but everybody calls me Greek."

"Hello, Jason." She shuffled her food and managed to free a finger, which he shook solemnly. "Are you from Greece?"

"No, he's a geek, but Greek sounds better," explained his companion, who also shook her finger. "I'm not so proud. Call me Moron."

"Moron?" Lisa repeated. "Isn't that an insult?"

"It's better than Nerd, which is what he is," Greek said affably. "A computer nerd."

"Besides, Moron beats Percy Moroni, which is my real name." On the point of rubbing his palms together, the thin-faced fellow stopped and regarded the hand that had touched Lisa's. "I'll never wash it again."

"You'll never wash what again?" said Greek.

Lisa ate a couple more fries. The boys stopped babbling and stared as the food went down her throat. It seemed to her that their gazes dropped well below the point at which her swallowing ended.

"Greek, you started to say something about Ginger," she commented when she was through.

"Oh! Yeah." His gaze wandered over the beach. "See, we've got this crash pad."

"You and...Moron?"

"And a few friends," added his pale friend. "Ladies welcome, anytime."

"Red hair and freckles? About sixteen? She might have been there, uh, one or two nights," Greek continued. "Is she in trouble?"

Lisa restrained the impulse to wolf down more food. For one thing, she needed to ask some questions. For another, she didn't enjoy having her digestive processes scrutinized.

"No," she said. "But I'm worried about her. Any idea where she is?"

Two heads jerked back and forth. No.

"We'll send her over if we see her," said Moron.

Not such a good idea. "Better yet, let me know where she is, okay? She's real jumpy. I just need to talk to her."

"Will do," said Greek.

"Where's your place, anyway?" she asked.

"You planning on paying us a visit?" asked Moron. "You're welcome anytime."

He started to give her the address, and then both boys began to fidget and twitch. Lisa wondered if they'd been attacked by sand fleas, until she realized they were staring at someone over her shoulder.

She turned. Toward them marched a stocky policeman with a black holster belted around his midsection.

The boys edged away. "It's Officer Nosy," Moron said.

Paper crinkled. Greek, she noticed, was clutching a paper bag in his left hand. As he tightened his grip, it took on the unmistakable shape of a wine bottle. Alcohol, she recalled seeing on a sign, was forbidden on the beach, along with unleashed dogs and fireworks.

''Gotta go,'' said Greek, and the two young men melted into the crowd.

Relieved to be alone, Lisa took a bite from her hamburger. It took a moment before she realized that the policeman had stopped, square in the middle of the sidewalk.

He was staring right at her.

Chapter Ten

Ryder should have worn sunscreen. As his watch edged past noon, he could feel the back of his neck frying, and his arms were turning suspiciously pink.

He'd figured that having a modest tan would protect him. He'd forgotten how much sand and water intensified the effects of the sun's rays.

An hour of distributing flyers and chatting with people might have toasted his skin, but it hadn't netted much information. Not many girls had Ginger's distinctive coloring, and a few people thought they'd seen her, but none could pin down a location.

The weather was hot for April, he reflected grumpily. If only they'd gotten rain, Ginger would be easier to spot in the deserted beach area. She might even have returned home on her own.

The canvas bag of flyers was nearly empty. By the edge of the sidewalk, Ryder paused to flex his back and gaze over the crowd of wall-to-wall beachgoers.

A red-and-blue disk whirled past him. A girl caught it, giggled, and heaved it back into the air, without even appearing to know who had thrown it in the first place.

Down by the surfline, a group of kids was building

a sand castle. Despite the stubby walls and crumbling turrets, their construction clearly soared in their imaginations.

The scene oozed peacefulness and safety. A sense of community, even.

To a pampered girl like Ginger, this must seem like one big playground. Ryder hoped she would have no reason to learn how dangerously deceptive beach life could be.

Among the throng, he spotted two people sitting on a towel, gazing out to sea. One had a mane of rusty hair spilling over her T-shirt. Ginger? Right there in front of him?

Cautiously he went to investigate, picking his way between discarded soda cans, umbrellas and sunbathers. He was three steps away when the redhead turned to frown at him.

Beaked nose. Stubbly cheeks. Sideburns. A guy, and not a particularly friendly looking one, either.

Ryder handed him a flyer and beat a hasty retreat.

The scent of fish frying in a seafood outlet reminded him that it was lunchtime. He ought to get back and check on Lisa.

It also wouldn't hurt to buy a bottle of sunscreen at the surf shop. Ryder could endure pain; sometimes he relished the sense of control that came from hanging tough. But suffering unnecessarily wasn't brave, it was stupid.

As he turned back, his thoughts flew ahead to Lisa. Would she still be there? Had he been a fool to leave her alone and give her the run of his friend's business?

She wasn't a thief, he reminded himself. If she were, she'd have taken the money in his wallet at the chalet. He didn't believe she was up to anything else underhanded, either.

More and more, Ryder admitted, as he stepped aside to let a skateboarder pass, he was beginning to believe her claim of amnesia. Everything she said and did fit the story.

Maybe he simply wanted it to be true. To believe that for a little while she belonged exclusively to him.

Even here at the beach, where young, scantily clad women abounded, no one attracted him like Lisa. It wasn't only her striking appearance, but something deeper. Intelligence, humor, warmth...

Ryder gave himself a mental shake. He'd escaped his father's aimless, impoverished life by never letting himself get soft. He didn't intend to start now.

On the sand near the walkway, a young woman struggled to open her beach umbrella. Ryder felt no compulsion to play Good Samaritan, but he wanted to give this new arrival a flyer, so he went over to help.

"Allow me." He reached for the recalcitrant shade.

From beneath a straw hat, a pair of sunglasses swung toward him and he felt himself examined critically. "Thank you." A measured tone. The woman, he realized at second glance, must be in her early thirties.

Taking a guess at why she was on vacation during spring break, he said, "You wouldn't happen to be a teacher, would you?"

A cautious nod answered him.

"I'm looking for a runaway." After snapping the umbrella into place, he took out Ginger's picture. The woman glanced at it.

"I've seen her," she said.   ·

"Where? When?"

"Yesterday afternoon." Frown lines fanned around her mouth. "Frankly, that's one of the reasons I came back today. I was worried about her."

"Why?" Ryder asked.

"Mind telling me who you are?"

He produced his investigator's license. After studying it, the woman said, "A man was talking to her for a long time. They were standing in an alley, and it looked as if he were trying to lure her away from the beach."

It was the kind of scenario Ryder feared most. "Can you describe him?"

The woman gave a frustrated sigh. "Medium height, medium coloring, about thirty-five, I guess. His clothes looked cheap—not casual or raggedy, but the kind of heavy polyester stuff you find in a thrift shop. He was doing most of the talking."

"How did she react?"

"She seemed uncomfortable but not frightened," the teacher said. "You know how teenagers are. They think they can handle anything."

"Did she leave with him?" Ryder prayed that the answer would be no. Not just because Anthony Callas was his client, either.

The woman shook her head. "He grabbed her hand as if to take her with him. It bothered me so much that I started toward them. Before I could say anything, he gave me a dirty look and left."

"Did you talk to her?" Ryder asked.

"The way she glared at me?" the teacher said. "I could see there was no point in giving her a lecture. I was just grateful she didn't go with that man."

He handed her a business card. "If you see her

again, I'd appreciate a call. Her father is very concerned.''

He returned to the walkway. By this time, the scent of seafood had become overpowering. Reasoning that he would need to stay at the store while Lisa went out for something to eat, Ryder purchased a paper boat full of fried clams.

They were greasy, chewy and a treat. He munched contentedly as he headed to the surf shop.

So Ginger had been alive and well on the previous day. Ryder could only hope the polyester man wouldn't return to try his luck again in the same place.

His steps slowed as he observed Lisa standing outside the store, hamburger in hand. Her long dark hair ruffled in the breeze, and the scarf wound around her head made her resemble a Gypsy beauty.

A policeman stood with his back to Ryder. From his stance, he seemed to be speaking intently, while Lisa's forehead puckered in confusion.

Were the authorities searching for her, after all? Were the New York police merely concerned for her well-being, or was she wanted for some other reason?

Ryder approached, keeping his hands in sight so as not to appear threatening. ''Can I help you with something, Officer?''

The patrolman shifted position so he could see them both at once. ''Are you this lady's boyfriend, sir?''

''Yes, I am.'' The truth, more or less.

''Has she seen a doctor for these injuries?'' He indicated the bruising along Lisa's face and shoulder.

''I told him I didn't need one,'' she interjected.

The policeman watched Ryder. The implication

was unmistakable. Abusive behavior had, at long last, become a serious concern to law enforcement, and the man was trying to make sure Lisa wasn't an unreported victim.

"Did you explain about the accident?" Ryder asked her.

She wore a puzzled expression. "I told him I got hit by a cab, but I don't think he believes me."

"We don't see a lot of cabs around here," the officer said mildly.

"In New York," Ryder said.

"New York?"

"She was hit by a cab at LaGuardia Airport." He saw no point in hiding the details, since the officer— J. Valencia, according to his name tag—was only checking out a case of possible battering. "She was treated at a hospital there. Lisa, show him the stitches."

"Oh!" Reaching up, she removed the scarf and leaned forward.

Officer Valencia inspected her head wound gravely. Unlike most of the men passing by, he showed no reaction to Lisa's feminine allure. "That does look like a professional job."

"Believe me, I don't hit women," Ryder said.

"Hit me?" Lisa gasped. "Of course not!"

"We can't be too careful," said the patrolman. "Women frequently deny it to protect their men."

"If a man ever hit me, I'd scratch his eyes out!" Lisa declared, so indignantly that even J. Valencia smiled.

Ryder decided the time had come to enlist some official help. "The truth is, we're here looking for a runaway girl." He displayed his license. "Her father doesn't want to make an official report, but I'd appreciate your letting me know if you see her.''

The policeman glanced at her photo and listened with concern to the account of the polyester man. ''We're restricted as far as taking minors into custody unless there's evidence of wrongdoing, but I'd be happy to notify you if I see her. And I'll certainly keep an eye out for that guy.''

Ryder gave him a business card. Officer Valencia tucked it in his pocket, wished them a pleasant afternoon and sauntered off.

''How peculiar,'' Lisa said. ''He thought *you* did this to me!''

Ryder gazed into her delicate face. He couldn't imagine anyone wanting to hurt her. Even when he'd been most furious with her, right after she dumped him, he would have risked his life to protect her.

''He was just doing his job,'' he said. ''You'd be surprised how many jerks there are in the world.''

Then something occurred to him. He and Lisa had both, instinctively, withheld information about her amnesia. As if they both realized it might be risky to involve the authorities in the search for her identity.

As if we were in this together, against the world.

Ryder scolded himself for exaggerating. Or, perhaps, for letting himself care too much.

''How did it go this morning?'' He gestured toward her food. ''Sorry I didn't get back earlier. I was planning to relieve you.''

''It went fine, but kind of slow.'' Lisa plucked a clam from his container and downed it appreciatively. ''I feel bad for Biff. We ought to help him drum up business.''

''I thought that's what I was doing.'' Ryder indicated his nearly empty bag of flyers.

They strolled toward the store together. ''That's true, but...'' As she opened the door, Lisa glanced toward the rack of coverups and women's swimsuits. ''Who would even know that stuff is in here, if they didn't come in to buy a surfboard? And how many women surf?''

''He's got a couple of bikinied mannequins in the window,'' Ryder pointed out.

''I thought they were just to attract attention to the surfboards. I didn't realize he actually sold women's clothing until I walked in for the first time.'' Lisa planted her hands on her hips. ''I've got it!''

''I'm afraid to ask what 'it' is.''

''An idea.'' She pushed him toward the counter. ''You take over the register. I'll be back.''

''What—''

''I don't know what line of work I used to be in, but something tells me I have a knack for promotions,'' she told him on her way out the door. ''See you!''

As it turned out, she wasn't so much seeing him, as he—and a lot of other people—were seeing her, Lisa discovered.

It hadn't taken long to snag her new friends from the previous day. Starr jumped at the chance to put on a fashion show, and Buffy couldn't resist coming along.

They changed clothes in the little dressing room and paraded in front of the store. The object was to attract women customers, but most of the gawkers were male.

Lisa could feel Ryder's irritation burning into her back from inside the store, but she refused to give up. Already several young women were wandering toward them to find out what was causing the fuss.

Neither Buffy, with her short brown hair and still-childish figure, nor tall, knobby Starr drew the same response as Lisa, but they giggled and whooped, having a good time. More girls approached, and several went inside to check out the merchandise.

It was working! Lisa felt a small thrill of satisfaction when she saw one girl emerge with a purchase in hand. She didn't know why she took such pride in bolstering Biff's sales, but already she was contemplating other promotional ideas. Perhaps a karaoke contest, or a Mr. Wet Suit competition.

If she never found out who she was, she might apply for a job with a marketing firm, Lisa decided. Or take courses in the field. She wanted to learn as much as she could.

When she ducked inside to change costumes, she saw Ryder ringing up a sale. He wore a long-suffering expression, but at least he didn't object when she put on a swimsuit and went out.

"That looks fantastic," Starr said after Lisa emerged in a scarlet one-piece with black racing stripes. "You really fill it out."

"How old are you, anyway?" piped up Buffy.

"I'm—" It struck Lisa that she didn't know her own age. The discovery gave her a moment of panic, as if she'd nearly stepped off a cliff. Hanging on to her composure, she said, "Over twenty-one."

"Yeah, I guess once you get up there, the exact age doesn't matter, huh?" said Starr.

Whatever Lisa might have replied was lost as she

caught sight of a new arrival among the onlookers. A girl with a froth of red hair and a generous sprinkling of freckles.

Standing alone, Ginger wore jeans and a T-shirt instead of swimwear like most other girls, and she was carrying an oversize shoulder bag. The earmarks of a runaway, Lisa supposed.

Until now, she hadn't considered what she should do if she spotted the girl. As Ryder had pointed out, it would only scare her away to indicate they were looking for her.

On the other hand, Lisa had told Buffy and Starr that she was seeking a friend named Ginger. At the moment, thank goodness, they were practicing graceful—well, almost graceful—turns a short distance away, and hadn't noticed the newcomer.

"You want to join us?" Lisa called impulsively. When Ginger didn't respond, she added, "You could try modeling!"

The girl made a face. "It's not my style."

"You won't know till you try."

Her lip curled into a sneer. "I wouldn't do it unless I got paid, anyway."

Mercifully, the crowd was thinning. Buffy and Starr wandered a few doors down, showing off their wraparound dresses to two lifeguards waiting in the hamburger line.

Lisa walked over to Ginger. "Hi, I'm Lisa."

"Who cares?"

"What's wrong?" Lisa said, looking at the girl with concern.

"I'm not a model type and everybody knows it." Ginger thrust her chin into the air. "Don't patronize me."

"You could do it as well as Buffy and Starr." Lisa indicated the other girls.

"Oh, please! Don't compare me to those dorks!"

The girl had a massive chip on her shoulder. No doubt it was covering up insecurity and vulnerability, but did she have to act so obnoxious?

"Is there anybody you *don't* dislike?" Lisa asked.

"I don't dislike them." Ginger adjusted her shoulder strap. "Or you, much."

"You could have fooled me," Lisa shot back. "I offered you a chance to have fun and you threw it in my face."

"How would you understand? Even all banged-up, you're still gorgeous." Ginger wrinkled her nose in disgust. "You have it easy."

Lisa knew better than to point out that there was nothing wrong with Ginger's looks. Or that she sounded petty and snide. Her goal was to persuade the girl to return home, not to chastise her. Or analyze her, either.

"You staying at the beach this week?" she asked.

"None of your business," Ginger retorted with a trace of nervousness, and turned away.

Lisa wanted to grab her, but she had no right to restrain the girl. Besides, it would only antagonize her.

A lifeguard vehicle jounced by on the sand. People moved out of the way, and in the shifting of the crowd, Ginger vanished.

Only then did it hit Lisa that she should have called Ryder the minute Ginger started to leave. She'd had their quarry in her sights and tried to handle the situation alone, and she'd blown it.

He was going to be furious.

Sick at heart, she went inside. Her two young assistants were still flirting with the lifeguards, and the only customer in the store finished browsing and left.

"You've done well," Ryder said. "We moved three sarongs, two bikinis, a sunhat and quite a few odds and ends. If Biff carried scarves like yours, we could have sold half a dozen."

"I saw Ginger," Lisa said.

He came to attention. "When? Where?"

"She stopped to watch us modeling." Lisa went inside the changing booth. While she stripped off the swimsuit, she related the conversation. "I'm surprised she can even move, with that massive chip on her shoulder."

He took a moment before answering. "She's obviously not ready to go home, but she doesn't exactly sound happy, does she?"

"Hardly." Lisa pulled on her own new dress. "I feel bad for her, but she's not very likable."

"Not around grown-ups, anyway."

"Ryder, I'm sorry." She emerged from the booth and faced him squarely. "I tried to hold my negative feelings in check, but maybe she picked them up. If I'd been nicer, she might have stayed. In any case, I should have called you."

He relaxed against the counter. "I'm glad you didn't."

"Why?"

"As far as Ginger knows, you're just a lady at the surf shop. Not oozing warmth, maybe, but someone she could talk to in a pinch. She might come back if she gets scared."

"She could call home," Lisa pointed out.

"Only if she were truly desperate. She might come to you if it hasn't yet gone that far."

A surfer entered to check out their selection of stick-on tattoos. After he bought a packet and left, Lisa said, "You never told me why she ran away."

"Last Friday, she had an argument with her father about grades. He admits he called her spoiled and lazy. When he got home from work, she was gone. She must have just packed and left."

"Like me," Lisa reflected. "At the chalet. But I don't think I was mad at you."

"And you found me again, hmm?" Ryder plucked a loose thread from Lisa's shoulder. "You're half-naked in that outfit, you know that?"

"It's perfectly respectable!" she protested. "It covers everything."

"Everything?" He ran a finger along the upper edge of the dress, tracing a fiery path across Lisa's cleavage. "Another few inches lower and you could nurse a baby."

Baby. An image stirred in the back of her mind. Could she have left a baby somewhere? Surely she wouldn't have forgotten *that!*

"Lisa?"

"I almost remembered something," she admitted. "About a baby."

"We quarreled about having children." He lowered his forehead until it touched hers. They stood so close she could see the sunburn on his nose. "I told you I didn't want any and it upset you."

"I like kids." Lifting her arms, Lisa draped them around his neck. "You'd be a terrific father, Ryder." She expected him to draw away, but he didn't.

"I chose not to think about it at the time, but maybe that's why you left."

"Because you didn't want kids? Did I make a big fuss about it?"

"No, but I could feel you withdrawing. At the time I figured it would pass," he murmured, his voice vibrating into her ear. "Maybe you gave up on me."

"Why are you so sure you don't you want children?"

"Because they tie you down." The answer slipped out so readily, it seemed automatic.

"So does anything you make a commitment to," Lisa said.

His forehead rubbed hers as he shook his head in disagreement. "Not the ways kids do. They need things all the time. Attention, money, discipline, new shoes. They're a bottomless pit. I don't have that much to give."

She bit her lip in dismay. Lisa felt strongly that she wanted a baby, and she wanted one with this man. *Was* that why she had fled?

His arms encircled her waist and he drew her hips gently against his. "On the other hand, making them could be a lot of fun. Are you sure you've forgotten what we did?"

Her blood heated like molten lava. "You could jog my memory," she whispered, no longer caring what deep-seated differences lay between them. Just as the past had vanished, so, in a way, had the future. Lisa didn't want to think about it.

Not when she could drink him in, experience the power in his shoulders, press her breasts against his chest and feel delicious sparks shoot through her. Not when his mouth was so close, closer, there...on hers, his tongue inside, his hands kneading her derriere.

"Excuse me? Could we change now?"

Lisa stumbled back. She'd forgotten about Buffy and Starr. "Oh, sure!"

Ryder made a low, growly noise and retreated behind the counter. His cheeks were flaming, or perhaps that was just the effects of his sunburn.

The girls hurried into the dressing room. Giggles drifted out. They were always chuckling about something, Lisa told herself, but this time she knew exactly what had inspired their mirth.

"To be continued," said Ryder. "Anyway, we *are* supposed to be working."

A short time later, the two girls and left. Opening his cell phone, Ryder called Ginger's father to report that the girl was unharmed.

"My associate has made contact with her," Ryder explained. So that's what she was, Lisa thought; his associate. "Miss Schmidt didn't identify herself as working for you. I think your daughter found her reasonably approachable."

He listened, then said, "Yes, we could knock on doors, but whoever she's staying with probably wouldn't tell us the truth. I think we'll have a better chance of reaching her if we wait for her to come back on her own. Of course, there's always a risk, so I'll leave the decision up to you."

After listening for a minute, he said, "I'm glad you agree. We'll notify you as soon as we see her again."

After he hung up, Lisa said, "He's really going to wait until Ginger comes by on her own? Now that we know she's in the area, I'm surprised he isn't hunting her down."

"What's the point of dragging her home if she just runs away again?" Ryder pointed out. "He needs her trust."

Lisa remembered what he'd told her earlier about the man in polyester. "What if that fellow shows up, the one in the alley?"

A muscle jumped in Ryder's jaw. "If he touches that girl, I'll strangle him with my bare hands. Now would you mind putting on a shawl or a sweater or something?"

She glanced down at her strapless dress. "What's wrong with this?"

"Not a thing. At least, not on the beach, where everybody reveals practically everything," Ryder said. "However, it's five o'clock and I'm not taking you out to dinner in an outfit that makes guys trip over their own tongues."

"You persuaded me," Lisa admitted cheerfully. "Dinner's the magic word."

She went into the back room to retrieve a cardigan she'd left there. At the same time, her thoughts flew ahead, past dinner to whatever came next.

Maybe they could finish the business that the girls had interrupted. Holding each other, awakening sensations that were new and yet familiar.

Making love with Ryder might bring alive memories of their previous time together. The prospect of experiencing him in two different ways at once was almost too intense to contemplate.

Double your pleasure, thought Lisa, and pulled the sweater tightly around her.

Chapter Eleven

Ryder had no idea what he'd eaten for dinner. It had been, he gathered from his empty plate, some denizen of the deep, swimming in garlic and butter, accompanied by crisp-steamed vegetables and boiled potatoes. It must have been delicious.

He was glad he didn't have to write a review of the ambiance, either. Low lighting. Mermaid murals, tacky but appropriate to the locale. Also, there was a waiter named either Jeff or Dennis.

He would have no trouble at all making an in-depth report on Lisa, however.

Eyes: as green as sea foam. Warm and vibrant.

Overall appearance: bruises invisible in the reduced light. Scarf adding a note of mystery. Hair a dark mass begging his fingers to comb through it.

Clothing: despite the sweater, the sarong remained provocative and tantalizing—make that maddening. Worse than the swimsuit, even. He couldn't help recalling that the sarong fastened with just a few snaps. It would take little dexterity, and even less time, to whip it off.

If only he didn't have such a sharp tactile memory of her body in the shower, writhing against his. Of her mouth melting beneath his kiss and her hardened nipples teasing his chest.

As the busboy carted off their dishes and the waiter appeared with a cart of desserts, Ryder felt himself growing ready for Lisa. Thank goodness for the heavy cloth napkin across his lap and the dim lighting.

"I'll pass," she told the waiter.

"Sir?"

"Me, too." No point in eating a bunch of calories he couldn't taste, anyway. "Would you bring our check, please?"

"Certainly, sir."

"How's your sunburn?" Lisa asked after the man left.

"It's formed a coalition with my ankle," Ryder said.

"You mean you hurt all over?"

"Something like that." He wasn't going to mention the keenest agony of all, the one in the middle.

"Do you have any balm at home?" Lisa asked. "We could stop at a pharmacy."

"I'm sure I've got something."

The check came, and he paid. They walked out into a cool, starry evening.

He'd left his car in the beach lot, several blocks away. The stroll raised protests from his ankle, but Lisa's peaceful nearness was more than enough to compensate.

As they neared the ocean, he saw firepits glowing against the sand and inhaled the smoky scent of barbecuing. On the darkened beach, a few shadows moved—most likely sunbathers seeking lost possessions, overzealous joggers taking a final turn and perhaps a few homeless drifters making a nest for the night. He wondered if Ginger was out there.

Maybe he'd been wrong to counsel Anthony Callas against hunting her down. Suppose she came to harm?

It wasn't Ryder's nature to worry unduly, however. If the girl were going to get into trouble, he told himself, she could just as easily do it in daylight.

They had reached the car when a blur of movement near the rear bumper sent adrenaline jolting through him. Pushing Lisa behind him, Ryder crouched in a martial arts stance.

A yowl split the night, and two cats raced past. With a hiss and another screech, they vanished across the nearly empty blacktop.

Silently Ryder cursed himself, not for sounding a false alarm but for dropping his guard. In his search for Ginger and his logic-defying ache for Lisa, he'd forgotten she might still be in danger. "Sorry," he told her.

"They startled me, too." She clung to his arm, though, he noticed.

Unlocking the car, he held the passenger door and felt Lisa's warmth as she passed him. A tendril of hair trailed across his cheek before vanishing.

With her safely tucked inside, Ryder took a moment to survey his surroundings. He saw nothing amiss.

If people were trying to harm Lisa, he felt almost certain that they'd lost the scent. In today's world, though, everyone left a paper trail. Sooner or later she would be found.

Tomorrow he would stay more alert. By then, too, perhaps her amnesia might lift.

Ryder slid into the driver's seat. "Anything come back to you today? From your past?"

Lisa considered. "Tulips!" she said abruptly.

"What about tulips?"

"They were in a flower box," she said. "Outside my room. Do people grow tulips around here?"

Ryder was no gardener, but one of his secretaries had talked incessantly on the subject. "They need a winter chill, which we don't get."

"I saw myself looking through the window at a flower box, but I couldn't see beyond it," Lisa explained as they drove away. "Tulips come from the Netherlands, don't they?"

"So I've heard," Ryder said. "Why didn't I think of it before? Schmidt could be Dutch. Ever wear wooden shoes?"

She made a face. "It sounds painful. What else do you associate with Holland?"

"Canals," he said promptly.

Her intake of breath cut through the air. "I can picture one! Running right down the middle of the street! And a glass-bottom boat going under a bridge!"

Ryder hadn't traveled much except for his stint in the Marines, but tracking people required some general knowledge of transportation. "To get there from New York, you would fly into Schiphol airport in Amsterdam, but your ticket was for Paris."

"Maybe I wanted to cover my tracks."

"You could have been planning to catch a connecting flight," he mused. "But where was the rest of the ticket? Unless you intended to catch a train or a bus."

"I don't know. None of it rings a bell."

The rest of the short trip passed in silence. Ryder didn't speak, mostly because he hoped Lisa might recover other memories. But if she did, she didn't mention them.

He drove past his carport and made a circuit of the parking area before returning. There was no sign of anything suspicious, but then, the safety lighting wasn't noted for its brilliance.

Ryder got out first and checked the area before he let Lisa join him. Then they walked quickly upstairs.

No sign of tampering greeted them outside the apartment. Inside, nothing had been disturbed, either.

"Did you just move in here?" Lisa asked, studying the beige blandness of the living room.

"Three years ago."

"Why haven't you decorated?"

"I hate clutter," he said shortly. "Besides, I'm saving my money."

"For anything special?"

"A house," Ryder admitted. "I never want to live the way my parents did. I want to own my own place."

She regarded him wistfully. "Won't it be awfully empty without a family?"

He'd never thought that far ahead. Besides, sentimentality wasn't Ryder's strong point. "I'll settle for peace and quiet."

Did she have to look so sad? Sad and seductive and breaking out in goose bumps from the dropping temperatures.

Ryder stroked her upper arms. "You're cold. That sweater's awfully thin."

"There has to be a reason for all this," Lisa said as if she hadn't heard.

"For what?" He drew her closer. Wanting to warm her. Aching to ease his own cold heart.

"Why I found you in the first place," she said. "And why I came back. I don't mean a motive, I mean—your business card was the only clue I had to my identity. It's as if I was *meant* to find you again."

"Dumb luck," he whispered as he brushed his cheek across her temple. The one that wasn't injured.

Her fingers feathered across his chest. "It feels so right, being with you."

"That's because we've done it before."

"Obviously, we should do it again." Her mouth came up to meet his.

Hot tickling pleasure spread through Ryder as the woman reverberated into his being. He wanted to take her slowly, to coast on the edge of ecstasy without letting himself go over. All evening. All night.

If he took forever to make love to her, then time would stand still. And Lisa would never have a chance to leave.

Her tongue explored the edges of his teeth. Taunting him. His hands caught her waist, and he felt the snaps of the sarong. How easy it would be to give them a tug.

His body registered delicious anticipation not only in his tightening groin but all the way down to his fingertips. Blood pulsed through his arteries in a teasing rhythm.

Ryder angled Lisa against him, no longer content to proceed slowly. What nonsense had he been thinking? He didn't want to wait; he wanted her fast and hard.

Never lose control. Never give in.

He was close to losing it now, even though he knew the risk he ran.

Two words on white paper. "Sorry. Lisa." Scraps in a wastebasket, too small to piece together. A chasm opening inside him.

He didn't want to need anyone that badly, ever again.

When Ryder drew back, he could tell from her dilated pupils and rapid breathing that Lisa shared his arousal. As cool air rushed in, she hugged herself to ward it off.

She didn't question him, or reach for him. Instead, she said, "You think I'm going to leave again."

When had she learned to read his mind? "Won't you?"

"I can't make any promises." She shivered. "It all depends on why I left in the first place."

"Care to offer a scenario that would justify your walking away?" he growled.

"If someone really is trying to kill me. And if they might kill you as well."

"I don't need protection!" Even as he spoke, Ryder knew it was useless. Lisa had withdrawn from him in spirit as swiftly as he had withdrawn physically. Or perhaps she'd held a part of herself back all along. "Don't do me any favors, Lisa."

"I'd rather stay," she said. "If you want me to."

A ruthless anger pushed him onward. "But you don't know what you left behind, right? Maybe you've already got a husband. Maybe..." But she'd been a virgin. Or had she tricked him? Such things could be faked, Ryder supposed.

Moisture glittered in her eyes. "You don't trust me, and I don't blame you. I'm not sure I trust myself."

He wanted to kiss away those tears and tell her he was sorry. To yield to his own traitorous emotions and forgive everything and let the future take care of itself.

Such a leap of faith wasn't in Ryder's personality. "Go to bed," he said.

Ducking her head, she hurried from the room.

He sat on the couch, his sunburn smarting unsympathetically. Ryder debated whether to stir himself and go into the bathroom. If only, among the contents of those cluttered drawers, he might find not only lotion for his skin but a balm for his bruised heart.

Grimly he plopped his feet on the coffee table and decided instead to anesthetize himself with television.

THE NEXT MORNING Lisa chose a pair of designer jeans and a blouse instead of the sarong. She'd tempted fate more than enough.

Thank goodness Ryder had stopped when he had. She'd wanted him with every cell of her body, and she knew she couldn't have exercised such self-control.

Two days ago, when she had nowhere else to turn, he'd rescued her. He deserved better than to be seduced and abandoned again.

She needed to get her own life straightened out before she could offer him anything. Or ask anything more of him.

In the meantime, Lisa vowed silently, as they drove toward the ocean, she was going to find Ginger and help Ryder earn his fee. She owed him that. Besides, however unlikable the girl might seem, she ran a terrible risk.

It was nearly ten o'clock, but the morning fog

hadn't yet burned off, and they found a parking space easily. "I'll get you settled at the store, and then I'm going to check out the food stands," Ryder said. "Ginger's got to eat somewhere."

Lisa remembered the two boys with the funny names who'd mentioned letting Ginger sleep at their place. In the encounter with the policeman and her impulsive decision to put on a fashion show, she'd forgotten them.

As they walked along the beachfront, she described the boys to Ryder. "Greek and Moron. It's weird that they'd choose those nicknames, don't you think?"

"Typical surfers," said Ryder. "They didn't happen to mention where their apartment is?"

Moron had been providing the address when he spotted the police officer, Lisa recalled. "He said the number, 125 1/2, and the street name started with a *P,* but he didn't finish it."

"The 'half' means it's upstairs," Ryder said. "The streets run at right angles to the beach, and the numbers begin at one hundred. That narrows it down."

"Do you know any names that start with *P?*" she asked.

His nose twitched in annoyance. "The streets around here are called after flowers. There's Pansy, Primrose and Poppy. Any of those sound familiar?"

"I just remember him saying 'P.'"

As Ryder let them into the shop, a delivery man scurried up with two cardboard boxes. He got Ryder's signature and departed at a near run.

"It's a good thing we were here to receive them," she said. "Did Biff mention he was expecting deliveries?"

"He said it was possible," Ryder noted. "If he's not in, they get left next door, so he wasn't worried."

After he left to check the food stands, she opened the first box. It contained goggles, nose clips and ear plugs, of which the store was running short. In the other box, she found Hawaiian-print skirts and halter tops.

Perhaps some of yesterday's customers would be interested in these designs. Lisa decided to put some of the clothes in the window.

Climbing into the narrow display area and dressing the two female mannequins proved a tricky job. By the time she finished, more than half an hour had passed and the sun was breaking through the clouds.

Outside, Lisa examined her handiwork. The bright-hued skirts and tops added a touch of class, compared to the skimpy bikinis they'd replaced, she decided.

About to go inside, she spotted two figures standing on the sidewalk half a block away. The girl had her back turned, but her red hair caught Lisa's eye.

It was the same length and texture as Ginger's.

The man fit Ryder's description of the creep in the alley—average height, medium coloring, wearing cheap but not shabby clothing. Early thirties, Lisa guessed, and noted a snake tattooed on his neck.

The way he kept edging toward Ginger, then backing away in a kind of dance, reminded her of a cat playing with a mouse. Then Ginger shifted, and Lisa saw that he was holding out a sack of fast food, as if it were a lure.

Ginger's fingers closed around the neck of the bag. The man caught her wrist, his eyelids flickering.

Lisa had never felt such a powerful sense of fear.

Not for herself, but for this girl walking blindly into the grip of pure evil.

"Ginger!" Lisa started forward, heedless of the heads that turned to watch. "Hey, wait up!"

The man glared at Lisa with such loathing that she wouldn't have been surprised to see venom shoot from his mouth. Mercifully, however, he released Ginger's arm and walked off.

The girl swiveled. Her reaction to Lisa was only marginally friendlier than the man's. "What do you want?" she demanded.

"Who is that guy?" Lisa asked as she jogged up.

"What do you care?"

She indicated the sack. "If you're hungry, I'd be happy to buy you something."

"I've already got food, as you can see." Ginger glanced toward where the man had disappeared. "You sure have a terrific effect on people. Do they always run in the opposite direction?"

"Only if they've got something to hide," Lisa said. "Why don't you come to the store and I'll make coffee?"

The redhead wavered, then scanned the beach. "There's some of my *friends*." She deliberately gave the last word ironic emphasis as she headed away.

"See you later."

"Only if I don't see you first."

Watching the girl, Lisa saw that she was aiming toward two wet-suited figures. Greek and Moron. At least they appeared harmless.

As she returned to the store, Lisa found that she was still trembling at the girl's close call. Yet Ginger didn't have a clue. She appeared to think any adult except the man with the snake tattoo was her enemy.

Lisa recalled a quote from Ginger's father, something about his daughter trusting anyone except the one person who cared about her. Well, the kid was running true to form.

Her agitation eased as she entered the store. For now, the man had departed. But he had approached Ginger at least twice. He was almost certain to return, because by now he knew that, if no one interfered, she might go with him.

It seemed like ages before Ryder returned. His expression darkened as Lisa described what she'd seen.

"I've got to call her father." He took out his cell phone. "As soon as I see Officer Valencia, I'll inform him about this, too."

Lisa kept busy dusting off a shelf as she listened to the one-sided conversation. She gathered that Anthony Callas was demanding they find Ginger again, at once.

When Ryder hung up, he said, "He's venting his anger on us. But he's got an urgent meeting and can't get here himself till this afternoon. Tells you something about his priorities, doesn't it?"

He smeared himself with sunscreen, then loaded his bag with a fresh batch of flyers and went out. They were both hoping, Lisa knew, that he could spot Ginger and keep her in his sights.

The morning passed slowly. Ryder popped in twice, only to report no news, and the girl didn't return to the store.

Several women came in to examine the new skirts and tops, and one made a purchase. Three surfers passed nearly an hour in examining a board, then departed promising to think it over.

Lisa spent a lot of time thinking about Ginger and

her father. She wondered when the girl had developed such a chip on her shoulder, and why the father hadn't taken time off work to search for her himself.

What were her own parents like? she wondered, and allowed her mind to wander. Gradually, a shadowy image formed of a large room that resembled a hotel lobby. There were two people in it, a man and a woman, but they seemed too distant and reserved to be her folks.

Was it a memory, or a scene from a movie? The more she struggled to focus, the blurrier it became, and finally she gave it up.

Near lunchtime, Buffy and Starr dropped by. Impressed with the new clothes, they offered to stage another fashion show.

"Maybe later." Lisa didn't want to be parading around when Anthony Callas arrived.

"Want us to get you something to eat?" Buffy asked.

They were very considerate, Lisa reflected. Quite a contrast to Ginger. "That would be great." She gave them money for an order of fried clams. Yesterday's sampling had whetted her appetite.

Shortly after the girls left, a dark figure appeared in the doorway. Squinting against the sunlight, Lisa realized it was Ginger.

She reined in her instinct to leap at the girl. Instead, she said casually, "Ready for that coffee?"

The hair shook, no. The girl stayed where she was.

"Are you okay?"

A long, unsteady breath. "You were right. That guy's a jerk."

"What guy?" Lisa walked to one side so the sun through the doorway no longer blinded her.

"The one I was talking to." Despite her freckles, Ginger looked pale. "Ned."

"You saw him again?"

"He, like, came to the place where I've been sleeping," she said. "I was playing cards with the guys and I told him to beat it."

"The guys?" Lisa hazarded a guess. "Greek and Moron?"

"Yeah." So Ginger *had* been staying with them the whole time. "Ned got real mean. He said he'd spent money on me and I owed him. Money! Like, a few meals!"

"He's a manipulator," Lisa said. "Those meals were bait."

"Yeah, well, I never figured he'd think I *owed* him something. For a little food that cost, what, ten bucks total? That's nothing!"

"Maybe not to him." She avoided revealing that she knew Ginger came from a wealthy family. Not yet, when trust was just beginning to form.

"So, like, I'm afraid he'll come back," Ginger said. "You're a grown-up. How do you get rid of a creep?"

"You have to stop accepting gifts," Lisa said. "If you can, pay him back for the food. Then keep making it clear that you want nothing to do with…"

The girl stared down the sidewalk in dismay. "I don't believe it!" With a hard, angry look at someone out of Lisa's sight, she fled.

If it was Ned, why hadn't Ginger come inside for safety? Lisa ran to the doorway to check.

The man marching toward her had probably never worn polyester in his life. Squarely built, his dark red hair fringed with gray, he wore his thousand-dollar suit with an air of command.

"Ginger!" Blocked by two women pushing baby carriages, he shouted after the girl as she vanished around a corner. The man dodged and took a few running strides, but had to halt again to avoid a collision with a bicyclist. "What's wrong with people around here?"

"Mr. Callas?" Lisa asked.

"Yes?" Unable to follow his daughter without trampling a flock of small children wearing matching preschool T-shirts, he glared at the teacher shepherding them.

"I'm Lisa Schmidt, Mr. Kelly's associate."

"Where the hell is he?" Ginger's father glanced around impatiently.

She could see where his daughter had learned her rudeness. "Searching the beach. I'll page him."

"*I'll* page him," the man snapped. "My daughter doesn't seem to be afraid of you, so *you* go after her."

"Yes, sir!" Lisa barely resisted the impulse to salute.

"Hurry!" He whipped a phone from his pocket as he marched inside.

On the sidewalk, Buffy and Starr ambled toward the shop, carrying paper boats of clams. "Do you know where Greek and Moron are staying?" Lisa demanded as they came within earshot.

"I have kind of an idea," Buffy said. "I mean, I saw them come out one time, and I think I remember where it is."

Since she had a partial address, Lisa figured she and Buffy ought to be able to put two and two together. "Starr, would you watch the store, please?

Just tell people I'll be back soon. And ignore the man inside. He's naturally grumpy.''

''What about lunch?'' the girl asked.

''Eat yours. Save ours.''

She and Buffy hurried away. After a couple of wrong turns, they arrived at a white box of a building with wrought-iron stairs leading to the second floor.

The door to 125 1/2 stood open. Music blared from inside.

''There?'' Lisa asked.

''Yeah.'' Buffy nodded. ''Do you want me to come with you?''

She couldn't put a young girl in a potentially dangerous situation. ''I'd prefer that you go back to the surf shop. When Ryder shows up, you know, the man who was with me yesterday, bring him here. Would you do that?''

''Got it!'' chirped the preteenager, and loped away.

As Lisa reached the top floor, she prayed silently that Ginger had returned. And that Ned hadn't.

When she reached the doorway, it took a moment for her eyes to adjust. Then she made out Ginger's huddled shape on the floor by a loudspeaker, lower lip thrust forward like a toddler having a temper tantrum.

''You phony!'' the girl shouted at her. ''You tricked me! You were working for my father!''

''What?'' Lisa said. ''I can't hear you.''

''You're a creep! Beat it!''

Lisa cupped her ear and pantomimed trying to hear. The ruse worked: Ginger turned down the stereo.

''I said—''

''That I tricked you,'' Lisa finished. ''You're right.

My friend Ryder is a detective, and he's been trying to find you. I'm just along for the ride.''

"I don't need my dad!" the girl snarled. "I can make it by myself."

Lisa bit back the impulse to point out that Ginger wasn't doing a very good job of it. That must be becoming clear by now, but the girl wouldn't appreciate hearing it.

"You're right," Lisa said. "You *can* make it by yourself."

"Is that supposed to be sarcasm?"

"Not at all." Making her way past a pile of crumpled clothing and sandy towels, Lisa perched on the edge of a sagging couch. "You're, what, sixteen?"

A reluctant nod.

"Which means in two years you'll be legally an adult," she said. "You can get a job or go to college, whatever you choose."

"Tell me something I don't know," Ginger sneered.

Lisa's temper began to fray, but she kept her tone level. "If you intend to be independent, you need to find out what you want from life. Then you have to work for it like everybody else."

The words echoed in some recess of her mind, as if she were speaking to herself. Her old self.

Lisa had the sense that just before the accident she had resolved to take charge of her life. But what did that have to do with using false ID and trying to get pregnant?

Get pregnant? Where had that idea come from?

"My dad doesn't think I'm good for anything." Anger and wistfulness warred in Ginger's voice. "What's the use?"

"You've done things backward," Lisa said. "There's no point in running away from your father physically. You need his help to get through school. What you ought to do is distance yourself mentally so you can ignore what he thinks and set your own goals."

A light flickered in Ginger's eyes. "I never thought of it that way. Like, I can keep my room and my clothes, and run away inside. Sort of."

Lisa didn't notice the dark figure in the doorway until she saw the girl's sudden alarm. This time, there was no defiance, no adolescent cockiness, only naked fear.

Anxiously, hoping she was mistaken, Lisa turned her head to focus on the new arrival. A cold slimy sensation ran up the back of her neck as soon as she saw him.

The man with the snake on his neck had returned. And he was closing the door behind him.

Chapter Twelve

Ryder reached the store within five minutes of being paged. He found Anthony Callas prowling back and forth like a caged panther, while the knobby girl named Starr sat behind the counter, studying the man's suit as if planning to make knock-off copies.

"Where's Lisa?" Ryder asked.

"What do you mean, where's Lisa?" snarled his client. "Where's my daughter? I'm paying you bloody well to find her, in case you'd forgotten!"

Ryder hung on to his temper. "Just tell me why Lisa isn't here."

Callas clenched and unclenched his fists. "Ginger was talking to her when I arrived. She ran off, and your associate went after her."

"So what are you complaining about?" Ryder said irritably. "It sounds as if Lisa had things pretty well under control. Any idea where they went?"

"Obviously not!"

"Buffy went with her," Starr put in. "Lisa asked her where Greek and Moron were staying."

Lisa wouldn't have dragged the kid into this mess unless she had good reason. "Does Buffy know their address?"

"Not exactly, but she's seen the place."

"Aren't you going to do something?" demanded his client.

Running around trying to pin down a partial address was likely to result in missed connections and unnecessary confusion. "They may be on their way back right now. I'll give them another ten minutes."

"You're just going to sit here?"

"I may stand." Ryder didn't enjoy sending the man's blood pressure through the roof, but he intended to abide by his own judgment, not take orders from a hysterical father.

"Oh, no." Starr's eyes widened as a small, brown-haired woman wearing a shirtwaist dress and pumps marched through the door.

"What now?" growled Callas.

"It's Buffy's mom. They were supposed to meet! Hi, Mrs. Grayson."

"Hello, Starr. Where's Buffy?"

"She'll be right back."

"She was supposed to be at the corner twenty minutes ago! I've been checking every shop she might have gone in." The woman frowned. "Starr, what are you doing behind the counter?"

"Oh, like, helping out."

"Since when do stores hire twelve-year-olds?" The woman turned toward Ryder.

"She's not working for me," he said.

"Why are you wasting your time on this chitter-chatter?" Anthony waved one hand furiously. "Kelly, get them out of here!"

Mrs. Grayson drew herself up. "I'll be happy to leave when you produce my child!"

"We have nothing to do with your precious Muffy,

or whatever her name is! There are serious matters at stake here!''

"Mr. Callas," Ryder said, recalling why Buffy had left. "This woman's daughter is doing you a big favor."

"What kind of favor?" Mrs. Grayson twisted the strap of her shoulder bag. "What's going on here?"

Visions of being charged with contributing to the delinquency of a minor were flashing through Ryder's brain when a voice from behind him chirped, "Hi, Mom! Oh, sorry, I forgot what time it is! But the dentist always makes us wait anyway, doesn't he?"

Her mother stalked forward, pointedly ignoring Anthony Callas, and grabbed Buffy by the arm. "This way, young lady. You're grounded for a week!"

"But I'm supposed to take him back there!" The twelve-year-old tried to wiggle free. "Mom, I've got this important mission!"

"Take me where?" Concern coiled in Ryder's stomach. Why had Buffy been sent to fetch him if everything was under control? "Did you find Ginger?"

"I'm not sure." Buffy's sandals slid across the floor as her mother dragged her out. "Lisa wouldn't let me go into the apartment."

"Who was inside?"

"I don't know."

Warning bells rang in Ryder's mind. What if the predator had returned? Lisa had no weapons and, as far as he knew, no self-defense training.

And he didn't know how to find her.

"Mrs. Grayson," he said, "I'm sorry, but I need your daughter's help. Just for a few minutes."

"Mister, I don't know who you are, or your friend

here either, but these girls are preteenagers. Got that?'' The woman roared like a lioness protecting her young. ''You have no business even *talking* to these kids! Starr! You're coming, too!''

Reluctantly the blond girl emerged from behind the counter. Buffy, halfway out the door, called, ''The address is 125 1/2!''

''What street?''

If she'd had claws like a cat, Ryder felt sure the girl would have dug them into the floor and left a trail of scratch marks. ''It starts with a *P!*'' She vanished through the opening.

''Is this how you normally do business?'' blustered Anthony Callas.

Ryder couldn't afford to waste time arguing. ''Outside!'' he rapped, and the other man hesitated only a moment before obeying.

Producing his key, Ryder locked the store behind them. Thank goodness, less than an hour ago he'd come across the policeman and told him about Ginger's latest encounter, so the man was up to speed.

''There's an officer who patrols this area on foot. His name is Valencia. Tell him we're looking for 125 1/2 on a street that starts with *P!* And tell him it's urgent!''

''I'm not the one who's being paid to—'' Callas stopped. Maybe he'd finally heard himself, Ryder thought, and realized whose responsibility this was. ''Yes, of course. Just find my daughter.''

As he hurried down the sidewalk, Ryder reminded himself that there was no reason to believe Lisa might be in danger. Just a gut feeling so strong he could hardly breathe.

He had worried about her decamping on him. He

had worried about someone from New York hunting for her. But it had never occurred to him that he might be throwing Lisa into the path of a predator.

At 125 1/2 Poppy Street, Ryder was greeted by an elderly woman doing aerobics. Circulars stuffed the mailbox of 125 1/2 Pansy, which had a For Rent sign in the window.

When he rang the bell at 125 1/2 Primrose, a mother fixing lunch for her children said she didn't know anyone named Ginger, Greek or Moron.

Was there another street that started with a *P?* Ryder broke into a run along the beachfront sidewalk. The names weren't in alphabetical order. He'd passed Marigold and Zinnia, and the next one he reached turned out to be Lily.

Beyond that, he discovered, lay Heliotrope. He was about to go in search of a map when Ryder spotted yet another street sign. Peony.

He sprinted to 125 and ran up the stairs. The door stood ajar, but as he approached, someone inside pulled it shut.

Without weighing the consequences, Ryder grabbed the knob and hauled full strength. A sudden gap revealed a hand on the inner knob, a roughened man's hand with a spider tattoo half-covered by an ill-fitting polyester sleeve.

Clearly, the man hadn't expected company. In the time it took him to clamp down, Ryder managed to wedge himself into the space and grab the man by his shaggy hair, pulling his head back.

If I've got the wrong apartment, boy, am I in trouble.

"Ryder!" It was Lisa, inside. "Thank goodness!"

"Let me go or I'm filing charges," growled the man. His hair felt greasy in Ryder's grasp.

"Please don't let him loose!" Ginger spoke between gulps of air. "He said he was going to make me sorry I ever gave him a hard time."

"I never did nothing." The snake on the man's neck bulged and squirmed.

"We told him to leave, but he came in and closed the door," Lisa said. "Isn't that some kind of crime?"

"The girl owes me money. I got a right!"

Footsteps creaked on the stairs outside. Ryder let out a long breath as he spotted Officer Valencia with Anthony Callas right behind.

He didn't let go of his quarry, though. "This man might be armed," he called as he shoved the snake man face first against the door frame.

Pulling out handcuffs, the policeman snapped them onto the man's wrists, then frisked him. He removed a wicked-looking knife from a belt sheath and gave a low whistle.

The officer pulled out his phone and called for backup. While still on the line, he checked the man's wallet for identification and relayed the information.

"Daddy?" Ginger edged out of the apartment. "Oh, Daddy!"

She flew into Anthony's arms. He caught her close, and Ryder could have sworn he saw tears in the man's eyes.

Lisa half smiled as she watched them. Ryder couldn't believe he'd let her walk into this kind of danger; she looked so fragile in her jeans and thin blouse. More than anything, he wanted to take her home and keep her safe.

"You can't charge me with nothing!" the hand-cuffed man bluffed. "I was just talking to these girls. I'll sue you for false arrest!"

The officer got off the phone. "Well, sir, it appears you're wanted for violating parole. That, plus being a convicted felon in possession of a concealed weapon...."

"A pocket knife? That don't mean nothing!"

Valencia fought to suppress a smile. "You ought to know they've tightened the laws in California for repeat offenders. I don't think you'll be 'talking' to any girls for a long time."

A police cruiser pulled up in front of the apartment. While two other uniformed men took their suspect to the station, Officer Valencia courteously interviewed all the witnesses.

Lisa bore up well, with only a bit of shakiness in her voice to reveal that she'd been through a frightening ordeal. When Ryder finally escorted her away, however, he could feel her trembling.

"Let's go home," he said.

"The store! I left Starr in charge."

"She's gone and it's locked," he said. "Don't worry about it."

"Thanks." Lisa sagged against him. Ryder, slipping one arm around her for support, didn't mind at all.

IN ONE BLINDING BURST of fear, Lisa had discovered what mattered most.

When she'd seen Ned come through the door, her chest had squeezed so hard she'd had to fight to think clearly, to devise some method of stopping this monster—a race to the kitchen for a knife, except she hadn't known where the kitchen was. A scream, but it had stuck in her throat.

All she'd been able to summon was a desperate, beloved image of Ryder.

Suddenly he'd been there, his face dark with concern as he'd jerked the door open and yanked Ned's head back. In that instant, Lisa had discovered that she loved him.

Not only for saving her, but for being what he was. Fierce and tender, wary and vulnerable. A man who would risk his life for her, even though she'd once abandoned him.

She would never leave again. No matter who she'd been, or what scheme she'd been involved with.

"I'm sorry," she said as they reached the parking lot.

"Excuse me?"

"For running away last time."

They made their way down a lane clogged with vehicles searching for a free space. "What brought this on?"

It occurred to Lisa that, kind as he was, Ryder might not welcome a confession of love. Certainly he didn't owe her any permanent arrangement. "I just— don't think I appreciated you properly."

He opened the car door and eased her inside. "Feeling confused? It would be only natural, after what's happened."

"Confused?" Lisa said. "I'm thinking more clearly than I ever have."

"'Ever' being the length of your memory, which is less than a week." He closed the door and came around.

Lisa had to laugh. As he got in she said, "You don't like to accept compliments, do you?"

"Were you paying me one?" He turned on the ignition and backed out, to the delight of a Jeepload of teenagers ready to take the slot.

"Let me make it plainer. I think you're wonderful," she said.

Dark brown eyes swept her. "Not all that wonderful. I had no business involving you in this case, especially not after I realized a predator might be after Ginger."

"You only involved me because I had nowhere else to go! Besides, I'm glad I could help." Something tickled the back of her brain. "I had a snatch of a memory earlier, but I'm not sure what it means."

"Oh?"

"Something about pregnancy. We did quarrel about you not wanting children, isn't that what you said? But this was different. It had to do with me getting pregnant, as if it were likely to happen soon."

His mouth tightened. "We forgot to use a condom. Are you telling me—isn't it too soon to know?"

"Since last weekend? I should think so. Maybe I was worried about getting pregnant," she said. "Ryder…"

"Yes?"

I love you. But I don't know whether you're ready to hear it. What she needed to do, Lisa realized, was to show him. "Are we nearly home?"

"Right this minute," he said, and pulled into the apartment complex.

When they stopped, she didn't wait to be helped out. She came around and took Ryder's hand, and barely let him lock the car before she tugged him up the stairs.

THIS WASN'T the self-conscious young woman who had plucked Ryder off a ski slope, propositioned him and then blushed at undressing. This woman felt confident about herself and her sexuality.

She wanted him. And he needed her with every atom of his being.

He was still reeling with the fear he'd felt when he realized she might be in danger. It was worse than being dumped, worse than being tricked. If Lisa had come to harm, Ryder wasn't sure he would have been able to bear it.

He'd never had much use for love. That hadn't changed. Yet he'd recently recognized a hollowness inside him that only Lisa could fill.

In the bedroom she didn't wait for his participation. Off came the blouse and the bra, as if she were eager to be rid of them.

He let his gaze linger on her parted lips and firm, inviting breasts.

She moved sinuously as she bared herself for his pleasure. Her skin glowed, and her eyes took on a luster that revealed her own growing desire.

She unsnapped her jeans and slid them down her hips, relishing her femininity, enjoying his response.

Ryder flexed his shoulders as power rippled through his muscles. His pants grew tight across his groin. He belonged inside Lisa, burning away the chill of separation.

Hands on hips, she shot him a teasing smile. Shrugging free of his shirt, Ryder came forward and caught her, pressing her hardened nipples against his chest as his mouth invaded hers. Her tongue tantalized his and her arms enveloped him.

Through the fabric of his pants, her hot center teased his masculine hardness almost to the point of ecstasy. A groan welled from his throat and he pressed her backward onto the bed.

As the water bed rippled beneath them, Lisa trailed kisses along his jaw. Her hands seized his buttocks and urged him on. Smooth flesh wriggled beneath him, intensifying the sensations, while her mouth played across his.

Her body opened to him, and he barely managed to undo his pants before plunging into her. Ryder heard her breathing quicken, along with his own, as they united into one molten creature on a field of flames.

If only he could hold this perfect moment, make the razor-edged pleasure last forever. With Lisa, he had found a perfect balance between the agony of anticipation and the glory of satisfaction.

She must have felt it, too, because a stillness invaded them both. Their mouths formed a seal, and her hands held his hips, and he felt himself swell inside her.

Despite their efforts to prolong this tranquillity, the water-filled mattress picked up the faint stirrings of breathing and circulation. The bed began to move rhythmically, as if of its own accord.

Ryder could restrain himself no longer. Carefully, by fractions of inches, he drew himself out of Lisa and then entered her again. This time he was in command, and she lay within his power, only the tip of her tongue alive against his teeth.

This self-control proved more than he could bear.

With primal urgency, he intensified his thrusting and felt Lisa's grip on him tighten.

Joy splashed over him, as he and Lisa shimmered together. They soared, arced across a rainbow, and, at last, sank blissfully into an exhausted slumber.

As LISA HOVERED on the edge of sleep that night, her mind played over her lovemaking with Ryder.

She'd developed a sense of belonging so strong that it overwhelmed even her curiosity about her past. She and Ryder were forging something new and precious.

They hadn't said a word. He hadn't spoken the words *I love you* and neither would she until she knew he was ready to hear them.

She gazed at the man beside her. He had fallen asleep on his back, angled toward her protectively.

Even at rest, he bore the signs of hard living, in the tightness of his jaw and that jagged scar above his temple. He bore other, invisible scars from his childhood, Lisa had gathered. His refusal to commit himself to anyone must have been a vital protective mechanism, and she couldn't expect him to abandon it easily.

She would give him the time he needed for trust to grow. However long that took, she intended to stay with Ryder.

Chapter Thirteen

Boris snatched a newspaper from the sidewalk kiosk and threw a few francs at the seller. Without waiting for change, he shook the paper open and stalked along the broad sidewalk, letting the Parisians dodge him as he read.

There was no mention of the phony kidnapping, thank goodness. The maid had assured Lothaire that the De La Penas had notified neither the press nor the police, and apparently she'd told the truth.

Boris's plans were progressing to perfection. When their daughter failed to return after last weekend, the De La Penas had readily believed his e-mailed tale of kidnapping.

They were prepared to deliver a ransom of $1.5 million on Monday. An isolated vineyard, which he could access by helicopter, had been agreed upon as the delivery point.

There was only one, not-so-small problem. The De La Penas insisted that their daughter be handed over in exchange for the money.

Lothaire, dispatched to Denver on the chance that she'd returned there, had had no luck finding the girl.

She hadn't contacted her friend Maureen, either, according to the woman's boyfriend.

Where the devil was Annalisa? What if she turned up at home, or didn't turn up at all? What if the maid, who had grown increasingly nervous once she realized what she'd gotten involved in, panicked and told her employers what she knew?

When his cell phone rang, Boris snatched it irritably from his pocket. "Well?"

"Mr. Grissofsky?" A tenor voice spoke in German-accented English. "This is Win Hoffer." Ah, the cameraman. "I couldn't get hold of Lothaire, so I thought I'd try your number."

Boris could feel sweat popping out on his forehead, despite the cool April air. "Has Miss De La Pena contacted your girlfriend? As you know, we are very concerned for her safety."

"No, but I just thought of something that might be useful. Since you're so *concerned*."

The last word dripped with sarcasm. Win Hoffer couldn't know about the ransom demand, but he'd obviously figured out that something sneaky was afoot.

Boris paused near an entrance to the Metro. Subway riders breezed up and down the stairs, none lingering long enough to hear his conversation.

"And what useful thing might that be?"

Win Hoffer cleared his throat. "Something worth more than Lothaire's been paying me, I should think."

Boris gritted his teeth. So Win had called him directly, not because he couldn't reach Lothaire, but because he thought he could squeeze more juice from a bigger lemon. Sourly he said, "Twice the usual, then."

"I've remembered someone who might know where she is," said Win.

Balancing the phone against his shoulder, Boris pulled out his electronic notebook and took down the name, phone number and address. Ryder Kelly, finder of missing persons.

Win explained that he had suggested, via his girlfriend, that Annalisa ask this private investigator to help her locate a suitable father for her baby. Since the man's office was in Los Ángeles and she had gone to Denver, Win had assumed she'd disregarded his suggestion.

"But it occurs to me that she might have been in touch with him at some point," the cameraman said. "Maybe he knows who she visited in Denver. If not, he might be able to help you trace her. That is his specialty, after all."

They had two days. Not a lot of time to find the girl, snatch her, and cart her off by private plane to France. At this point, Boris would take whatever help he could get.

"If he finds her, it's worth triple," he said.

A CORPORATE EXECUTIVE had vanished with a computer disk of industrial secrets, and the head of the company wanted to meet with Ryder in an hour. He had a busy weekend ahead of him.

He finished returning the rest of his phone calls and chucked the last of his mail, mostly advertisements, into the round file. Another half hour and it would be time to leave the office for his appointment.

Lisa had insisted on being dropped off at the store

this morning, since Saturdays were Biff's most lucrative time. An edge of uneasiness had moved through Ryder as he watched her stroll away along the beachfront sidewalk, key in hand.

What had passed between them last night still glistened with such newness that he hated to let her out of his sight. He wanted to stay where he could watch expressions dance across her face and hear her laughter.

Now Ryder toyed with the idea of postponing the appointment, dropping by the beach and persuading Lisa to accompany him to some remote spot for the rest of the weekend. But this corporate case had a large bonus attached. Added to his savings, it would finally provide him enough for that down payment on a house.

The phone rang. Zizi, who was working on Saturday to make up for missed time, answered. A moment later she announced a Mr. Smith, calling from Paris.

Due to his Web Site, Ryder received a fair number of international inquiries, although not usually from men named Smith. Unless they wanted to hide their real identity, of course.

"Kelly here," he said.

"Ah, Mr. Kelly." A heavily accented voice. Eastern European, unless he missed his guess. "I am seeking my fiancée, who has disappeared in America."

"Think you could narrow it down a bit?" he asked.

"Her name is Annalisa Maria Von Schmidt De La Pena," the voice continued. "She is most beautiful, with long dark hair and green eyes."

Ryder's breath caught in his through. It was Lisa, almost without question. "How did you get my name?"

"You are a finder of missing persons, are you not?"

Not this one, he wanted to shout. "How long has she been missing?"

"A week, more or less." The man had a sibilant way of speaking that irritated Ryder.

"You say she's your fiancée?" *Then why did she choose me to take her virginity?*

"Does it matter?" snapped the man. "I need to find her, and I will pay well. Have you heard from her?"

"Heard from her?" Ryder repeated. "Why would I have heard from her?"

"It is complicated," the man said. "The girl is, er, on medication and has become disoriented. We believe someone gave her your name. Either you have heard from her or you have not, Mr. Kelly. Which is it?"

Ryder had no intention of handing Lisa over to this man, but at the same time the fellow obviously knew her real identity. He needed to learn more.

"Yes, I've heard from her," he said.

"When?"

"The last day or so."

"Is she in Denver?"

A red flag went up. How did this guy know Lisa had been in Colorado? Had he been tracking her? Was it possible he might have some connection to her accident in New York?

"I'm not sure," Ryder said. "She's supposed to call me again on Monday."

"Monday?" The man's voice rose until it nearly cracked. "We must find her at once!"

Ryder tensed at the fellow's obvious alarm. "Is she in danger? From this medication or...anything else?"

"Yes!"

"Then I should notify the authorities."

"No!"

Ryder's skin prickled. His instincts shouted that Lisa *was* in some kind of peril, and that it was because of this man. "I'm afraid I have no way of locating her immediately."

"What did she ask of you? Did you put her in touch with someone in Denver?"

"That's confidential," Ryder said. "It would help if you could tell me more about your fiancée. Is she ill? Is there family that should be notified when I locate her?"

Mr. Smith suffered a fit of coughing.

"Exactly where does this Miss De La Pena live, anyway?" Ryder glanced at his watch. Eleven o'clock. If he didn't leave soon, he'd be late for his appointment.

"I must consult with a colleague before we continue this conversation," said Mr. Smith.

"Fine with me." If she were his fiancée, why did he need to consult a colleague? Ryder wondered, his doubts growing even stronger.

"You will be hearing from me, Mr. Kelly." It sounded like a threat.

Ryder hung up with a sense of foreboding. Instead of resolving the issue of Lisa's identity, this Mr. Smith, or whatever his real name might be, had complicated it further. What on earth was going on?

Perhaps, presented with her real name, Lisa would finally remember some key facts. Ryder itched to drive to the beach and confront her immediately, but that would have to wait.

He had an appointment to keep. The corporate runaway's trail would grow cold if Ryder didn't get on it immediately.

Besides, what was the hurry? Even if Mr. Smith decided to fly to L.A., he couldn't get here from Paris until early tomorrow. There would be time enough after Ryder picked up Lisa this evening for them to hash things through.

Suppressing his anxiety, he collected a sports coat and tie and emerged from his office. At the front desk, Zizi clicked away at her computer, updating the accounts.

"Good luck with your date tonight," he said.

She waved and went back to typing. The woman might turn out to be a decent secretary, after all, Ryder reflected as he left.

As he got in his car, he heard the office phone ringing. Well, if it was important, Zizi would either page him or give the caller his cell phone number.

He couldn't afford to stop and check. Corporation presidents didn't like to be kept waiting.

THE YOUNG MAN had such a pleasant voice, with a touch of a Continental accent, that Zizi wished he were calling for her. But he asked for Lisa, although he tacked some Spanish-sounding name after Schmidt.

"Oh, she's at the store today," she said. "The surf shop." Only after she'd given him the address and hung up did she stop to wonder who the man was.

Maybe she ought to advise Ryder. Zizi was reaching for the phone when it rang again.

"Hi, it's Tom." Her date for tonight, the script reader. "I've got tickets to a press preview of one of our new films, and I wondered if you'd like to see it instead of going dancing."

A press preview? It sounded glamorous and full of possibilities. "Wow! Great! So, what's the film about?"

By the time she hung up, Zizi's brain buzzed with anticipation of the evening ahead. She forgot all about the young man with the Continental accent who was looking for Lisa.

CUSTOMERS KEPT the shop busy until late afternoon, when a surfing competition on a neighboring beach lured away most of the crowd. Resting her chin on one hand, Lisa sat behind the counter and gazed through the tinted windows at the sparkling ocean.

She'd resigned herself to spending the day away from Ryder, knowing he had to catch up at the office. But she hadn't realized how empty the store would seem without the vibrant knowledge that at any moment he might appear.

Restlessly, she went to reorganize the racks of clothing. Customers frequently stuck the sizes and colors back in the wrong place, and it took a while to reorganize them all.

When she was done, Lisa paused in front of the full-length mirror and studied the skin exposed by her sarong-style dress. Her bruises had faded, and dark hair covered the stitches on her scalp. She would need to get someone to take those out, she mused, and then she'd be as good as new.

A scraping noise from the back of the shop startled

her. It might have been in the storage area, but more likely it came from the alley that ran behind.

Lisa listened harder, but made out only the low rumble of the ocean. What she'd heard must have been children playing in the alley.

If Ryder couldn't be here, she wished she at least had someone to chat with. Buffy and Starr hadn't been around all day.

Abandoned by my friends, Lisa thought wryly. Just like Nicola.

Nicola. A face jumped into her consciousness: high cheekbones, wide-set eyes, chestnut hair threaded with silver.

Lisa clasped her hands together to control the excited trembling. Memories, at last!

Now she could see other faces. Her mother and father. A friend named Maureen. It was as if they'd been lurking in the shadows of her mind all week and had simply stepped forward.

What if she forgot again? Thrilled but a little anxious, Lisa hurried to the counter and drew out a pad.

She began to write the data as it came to her, in fragments. She remembered Maureen's phone number, but not her own. The location of the château, but not the address of the apartment in Paris, although she'd lived there longer.

Without intending to, she found herself jotting, "I came here to get pregnant so I wouldn't have to marry Boris Grissofsky."

Lisa stared at the words in dismay. Not so much because of the impending marriage, which she had no intention of entering. But because she now realized the depths of her betrayal of Ryder.

How could she have done this? True, she hadn't

known him when she'd begun her adventure. But it was terribly wrong to use another human being this way.

She might be pregnant right now, and it wouldn't be an accident. Ryder had made it clear he didn't want children. She had no right to do this to him.

Pain knotted inside Lisa's chest. It was hard to imagine that she had ever been that heedless girl who set out on a lark and ended up possibly changing everyone's lives—including hers and Ryder's.

She would have to tell Ryder everything. If he rejected her, she wouldn't blame him.

She could only hope he might be willing to work through this situation with her. It seemed like a lot to ask.

A draft of air played across Lisa's neck. Something was moving behind her. Something that wasn't supposed to be there.

"What—?" She started to turn, when one hand seized her shoulder and a cloth clamped over her mouth. Chemical fumes shot into her brain and everything whirled madly until the light began to dim.

Lisa glimpsed a man's face, youngish and clean-cut. She didn't remember him, not even a little.

The darkness sucked her inside itself.

THE MISSING EXECUTIVE didn't stay missing very long. He'd used his charge card to book a flight to Washington, D.C., and had telephoned his own home from a hotel, presumably to pick up messages.

Ryder traced the call and learned that, from the same room, he'd also called several rival companies, apparently intending to sell his information to the highest bidder. Stupid, Ryder thought.

The man should have lined up his ducks before he put himself in jeopardy. Right now two security officers and a top executive from the corporation's Baltimore office were en route to the D.C. hotel to confront the man.

If he handed over the disk and signed legal documents admitting guilt and swearing secrecy, they would quietly let him go. The goal was to prevent a scandal that might upset stockholders. And, of course, to keep trade secrets from falling into rival hands.

In the impersonal glare of the corporation's lighting, with the computer screen tirelessly meeting his demands, Ryder failed to notice the dusk lowering outside. Not until he stood up to accept the president's thanks did he notice that it was nearly six o'clock.

An hour late! The store must have closed by now. Why hadn't Lisa paged him?

Maybe she'd decided to pick up some dinner and hang out with her young friends, Ryder told himself. Then he remembered that Buffy was grounded.

When his cell phone rang, a surge of relief ran through him. Lisa must be checking in at last.

"Take your call," said the company president. "I'm getting out of here, but I've put through the approval for your bonus to be issued first thing Monday."

"Thanks." He whipped out the phone as the man departed. "Kelly here."

It wasn't Lisa's voice, but a masculine one. "Mr. Kelly, this is Officer Valencia. I thought you should know that I found the door to the surf shop unlocked but no one is inside."

Ryder struggled not to panic. "Lisa was there today. Maybe she's grabbing a bite to eat down the block.''

''I checked the area. There's no sign of her,'' the officer said.

''Did you look in the back of the store?'' She might be taking a nap, or perhaps she'd had an accident, Ryder thought frantically.

''Yes, sir, I did. She's not there, but I found a rear door open. There are scratch marks on the lock.''

Someone had broken in? ''I'll be there as soon as I can.''

As Ryder drove to the beach, one thought kept recurring. What if Mr. Smith had lied about being in Paris? He might have been in Los Angeles all along.

Lisa could have gone of her own free will, but she wouldn't have left the store open. And there had to be an explanation for the scratch marks on the lock.

At the store he found the police officer waiting. ''I'll be glad to file a burglary report if anything's missing, sir.''

Ryder stared around the shop. Not a surfboard out of place. When he checked the cash register, it bristled with cash, checks and credit receipts. ''The only thing that's missing is my girlfriend.''

The last time she vanished, she had left a note. Ryder almost hoped that he would find one, just so long as he knew she was safe.

''There are no signs of a struggle,'' the policeman said sympathetically. ''I've talked to the neighbors but no one reports hearing or seeing anything.''

If Lisa had left a note, it would be near the register. With a frown, Ryder noticed that a small box, offering the store's business cards, had tipped over and spilled its contents across the counter. How had these been knocked over?

As soon as he brushed away the cards, he saw a pad covered with scribbles. It wasn't addressed to him; it didn't appear to be a message at all, just random notes.

First came the names of two women, Nicola Dupin and Maureen Buchanan. Beside Maureen's name was a phone number with an international dialing code.

Next appeared the names Schuyler and Valeria Von Schmidt De La Pena and an address in France. De La Pena, he thought. Relatives, maybe parents.

So Lisa's memory had begun to return. Ryder's throat clenched. That would give her a reason to walk out, to resume her old life.

He pushed aside another card and saw scrawled at the bottom of the page: "I came here to get pregnant so I wouldn't have to marry Boris Grissofsky."

A dark heaviness settled into his stomach. So that was her game. Ryder couldn't imagine why she would need to get pregnant to avoid a marriage, but it explained Lisa's seduction of him.

According to Mr. Smith, someone had given her Ryder's name; it didn't really matter how she'd come by it. The fact was that she had flown to Colorado to use him as a human stud. After he'd fallen for her, she'd gone her merry way.

Only amnesia and chance had sent her back. Now she'd departed once more, possibly carrying his baby.

His baby. The prospect hit Ryder like a blow. His child. To grow up where? To be told what lies about him?

He'd never wanted to be trapped into fatherhood. Now that the possibility of a child had become real, however, he resented even more strongly being shut out of the picture.

"Mr. Kelly?" Office Valencia emerged from the storage room.

"Yes?"

"Do you recognize this?" He held out a sandal.

Ryder's heart thudded as he took it. It was a woman's shoe, about Lisa's size. A few scuff marks on the sole indicated that it had been worn, but not much.

"My girlfriend bought a pair of these two days ago," he said.

"I found it on the floor in the back," the officer said. "There's no sign of the mate."

Why would Lisa have abandoned one sandal? Why would she have left these incriminating scribbles—with enough information for him to track her—if she intended to disappear? It also made no sense for her to jimmy the lock and depart via the back door when she had a key to the front.

Ryder recalled Mr. Smith's Eastern European accent. It would fit a man by the name of Boris Grissofsky. Lisa had been willing to seduce a stranger to get away from him; she must have had good reason to dislike or even fear the man.

"Would you like me to put out an all points bulletin?" asked the policeman. "At this point I think we have enough reason to suspect foul play."

"Absolutely." After providing as much information as he could, Ryder went back to the counter and tore off the note.

He dialed the number for Maureen Buchanan, but no one answered. Despite struggling to communicate with several French operators, he couldn't find a list-

ing for the De La Penas at their address, which was
in the Loire Valley. Whatever information they might
be able to provide, he couldn't afford to wait for it.

He had to take action. He couldn't leave Lisa in
the hands of her abductor.

Lisa and our baby.

If she were in Los Angeles, the police had as good
a chance of finding her as Ryder did. But from everything he'd learned, he suspected she was being
taken out of the country.

It didn't seem likely that Grissofsky planned to deliver her to her parents. On the other hand, they were
apparently forcing her into a marriage, so they must
have some knowledge of this whole business.

It went against Ryder's nature to fling caution aside
and head blindly to France, to an address in the Loire
Valley that might not even be hers. Besides, now that
Lisa's memory had returned, he didn't know how she
felt toward him, or what kind of person she really
was.

She'd tricked him, shamefully, about the baby. But
how could he abandon the woman he loved when
there was a chance she needed him desperately?

Ryder felt himself hovering on a precipice. It was
the cliff that lurked in his nightmares, beyond which
lay a free fall.

Once he jumped, there was no telling where he
would land. It no longer mattered. He hadn't given
away his heart; it had left him, and he might as well
throw the rest of himself after it.

Picking up the phone, he booked the first flight to
Paris.

Chapter Fourteen

Lisa awoke to stiffness, darkness and the hum of an airplane. As if retaining fragments of a dream, she recalled being jostled and carried and plunked down.

How much time had passed? Where was she?

The last thing she recalled clearly was sitting at the counter in the surf shop. Hearing a noise, starting to turn, and her arm hitting a box of the store's business cards. Then...nothing.

Feeling a prickling sensation in her hands, Lisa realized they were tied behind her back. She couldn't see, and when she moved her head, she felt the tug of a blindfold.

Beneath her lay a rough blanket. Through it she could feel the floor vibrating as the engines churned.

Her nose wrinkled at the scent of cigarette smoke. It was too harsh for American tobacco.

The scent evoked a holiday in Greece with her mother. They'd eaten lunch at an outdoor café on the island of Mikonos, and the man at the next table had been smoking.

Her mother. Greece. The château. Her father.

She remembered everything, Lisa realized. Everything but the events of the past few hours.

Someone must have kidnapped her and taken her aboard an airplane. Boris. It had to be him. But why would he go to such lengths?

He'd been eager to set a wedding date. Was there some more pressing reason than mere impatience?

Maureen had said something about Win's camera work for Boris that Lisa hadn't paid attention to at the time, but now it came back to her. "The first check bounced."

Tycoons didn't write rubber checks. Not unless they'd run into serious trouble. Serious enough for her large dowry to become a major attraction.

Tears burned Lisa's eyes. She had no idea what Boris planned for her, but she knew that he'd made a terrible mess of her life.

Ryder. Her need for him ached like a physical wound.

He would assume she'd abandoned him. To make matters worse, if her abductor had left the notepad there, he would discover her notes and learn that she'd sought him out to get pregnant.

He would never forgive her.

No matter what it took, she would return and try to explain. But Ryder had struggled to find the heart to give her a second chance. A third one was inconceivable.

Lisa's muscles throbbed from her uncomfortable position, and the cigarette smoke stung her nose. Cautiously she began to work her wrists behind her back, but every movement made the ties bite more deeply into her skin.

She transferred her attention to the blindfold. By rubbing her cheek against the coarse blanket, she worked up enough friction to shift the cloth a fraction of an inch. Then another.

Frustration nearly made her cry out, but she didn't want to attract the attention of whoever was smoking. Since her feet weren't bound, Lisa moved them carefully, shifting until she hoisted herself into a sitting position.

Scooting backward, she bumped into a hard, flat surface that felt like a wooden crate. She brushed her cheek along it until something caught the edge of the blindfold.

Several tugs loosened it, and it slipped down onto the bridge of her nose. Squinting in the unaccustomed glare, Lisa surveyed her surroundings.

She was sitting in the back of an airplane, among boxes and crates. It was too small to be a commercial airliner, but large enough to be a charter craft or private jet. In the front a bulkhead cut off sight of the cockpit, and of whoever was smoking.

Light filtered through windows on either side. Pushing against the crate, Lisa worked her way toward a standing position. Her thigh muscles strained and nearly gave way, and she scraped her arms repeatedly, but desperation finally propelled her upright.

At first, she could see only sky through the nearest double pane. Apprehensively she craned her neck, and still she saw nothing but a vast sweep of blue.

Water, all the way to the horizon. They had left America. Even though she had been there only a short time, Lisa felt as if she were being dragged away from home.

Something rustled toward the front of the plane. Her heart jumped into her throat.

She heard a low exhalation, and then the sounds of

someone moving toward her. Instinct warned her not to let the man see that she was awake, but with her hands tied, she could do nothing.

Only stand there with her heart thundering and wait to see the face of her captor.

RYDER FINALLY got through to Maureen Buchanan from JFK Airport. She recognized his name and listened intently as he sketched the situation.

"Oh, Lord, this is my fault," she said when he paused. "I'm the one who put her up to this crazy adventure. But I can't imagine who would kidnap her, eh?"

Ryder described his phone conversation with Mr. Smith. "Could he be this Boris Grissofsky?"

"I suppose so, but—he told you someone had given Annalisa your name?" Maureen said.

"That's right." He stifled a yawn. It was early morning, and he hadn't slept much on his red-eye flight from L.A.

"Only three people knew about you." She sounded grim. "Me, Lisa—and my boyfriend, Win. He knows Boris, and he always needs money, but I never dreamed he would stoop so low as to spy on me. Why, that rotten..."

Ryder interrupted with questions, but Maureen had no idea where Boris might take Lisa. She did, however, provide him with a phone number and directions to the De La Penas' château.

As soon as he hung up, Ryder dialed the number. While it rang, he tried to imagine the place where Lisa lived, but all he could picture was Sleeping Beauty's Castle at Disneyland.

A man answered in French, announcing the name

of the château as if he were either a butler or a tour
guide. Ryder, trying to summon up his slim high-
school knowledge of the language, came up with *"Je
m'appelle Ryder Kelly. Il faut que je parle avec Monsieur ou Madame De La Pena."*

He was feeling proud of himself, until the man
launched into another question which Ryder couldn't
begin to understand. In English he fumed, "It's about
their daughter! Get moving!"

"One moment, *monsieur.*" Ryder heard the man
pace away, and then voices echoed as if in an enormous chamber.

Another man came on the line. He sounded less
imperious but more impatient. "What about my
daughter?"

"My name is Ryder Kelly. I'm a friend of hers, a
private detective from Los Angeles," he said. "Lisa's
been kidnapped."

"Yes, we know that."

"You do?"

"We've been in touch with her kidnappers for several days."

"That's impossible," Ryder said. "She was only
abducted yesterday."

"What kind of game is this?"

"You can contact the Beachside, California, police
if you don't believe me," he persisted. "Look, Mr.
De La Pena, Lisa has spent the last week with me. I
believe she's been abducted by someone named Boris
Grissofsky."

The sound that emanated from the phone lay somewhere between a snort and a snarl. "How dare you
insult a relative of the Hohnersteins? A man of impeccable character and breeding!"

"Breeding?" No wonder Lisa had treated Ryder as a stud, since her father talked about people as if they were cattle. "Listen to me—"

"No, *you* listen to *me,* Mr. Kelly. I don't know who you are but you have no right even to be in the same room with my daughter, let alone insult my future son-in-law!" roared Schuyler De La Pena. "I can smell a fortune hunter a continent away. If you ever trouble us again, I'll see you in prison!"

The line went dead abruptly. Lisa's father had hung up on him, which made his stomach burn.

Lisa didn't just come from a wealthy family, she came from a den of snobs who believed that being related to the Hohnersteins was proof of good character. And that not being a member of their elite "club" made you worthless.

Lisa obviously did not share their blindness, or she wouldn't have fled Boris Grissofsky in the first place. Still, in the long run, how could Ryder hope she would be satisfied with the kind of modest life he could provide?

Then he remembered the baby. The one she might be carrying. His.

With all his soul, Ryder had rejected the prospect of bringing up children in poverty. Well, it was time to let go of outdated fears.

He wasn't poor anymore. He might never own a château, but there were worse things for a child than growing up in a modest house in a Los Angeles suburb.

Like living with parents who considered their daughter some kind of broodmare.

Now to the puzzle that Schuyler had presented when he declared the kidnappers had contacted him several days ago. Apparently Boris had taken advantage of Lisa's disappearance to demand a ransom. As the time came to turn her over, he must have seen the need to snatch her for real.

Ryder didn't know all the details, but he felt certain that Lisa's life was in danger from the very man her parents trusted. Any number of things might go wrong with the ransom attempt.

What if Boris decided to up the stakes at the last minute? What if Lisa recognized her abductor and threatened to expose him?

The loudspeaker blared an announcement of the departing flight to Paris. This was Ryder's last chance to withdraw.

Inside him, the ghost of a little boy shuddered at the prospect of facing a châteauful of aristocrats. Of weathering once again the kind of cruel sneers that had haunted his adolescence. Of risking his life for a woman who had sought him out because she wanted a faceless stud to get her pregnant.

The images faded before the memory of Lisa, her eyes aglow when he'd rescued her and Ginger. Fragile and determined, buoyant with relief, needing his arms around her. Which was exactly where he wanted to put them.

Briefcase in hand, Ryder strode to the departure gate and left his ghosts behind.

SHE DIDN'T KNOW this man.

Lisa had been so certain that Boris had kidnapped her, that she thought for a moment this other man must be the pilot. Then she remembered his face from the surf shop, the moment before she passed out.

He was in his twenties, smooth looking except for

a few acne scars. The brown hair and short mustache were clipped with military precision, the dark suit smartly tailored, the tie perfectly flat.

The cold perfection of the man frightened her. Lisa sensed immediately that she wouldn't be able to enlist his sympathy. "Who are you?"

His nostrils flared. "You weren't supposed to see me." Then he shrugged. "My name is Lothaire Warner. I work for Boris Grissofsky."

"Where are you taking me?"

"To your parents." Lothaire approached with measured steps. "If you give me your word you won't fight, I'll cut your hands loose." When she hesitated, he added, "It's not as if you can escape. Or get help. There's no one on board but you, me and the pilot, and he does what I tell him."

"Boris isn't here?"

He let out a low, humorless chuckle. "That idiot? He's waiting at a private airport outside Paris."

Boris an idiot? At least she and Lothaire agreed on that point. "Okay, cut me loose."

From the pocket of his impeccable suit, the man plucked a thin, deadly knife. An instant later, the bonds dropped from her wrists.

Blood stung her palms and fingers as it rushed back. She flexed her shoulders and tried not to wince as the muscles spasmed.

The man stepped away. He hadn't even touched her, Lisa realized. "Why did you kidnap me if you're just taking me to my parents?"

"Because they are going to pay a rather large ransom." Leaning against a crate, Lothaire trimmed one of his nails with the knife.

"Does Boris know about this?"

"Absolutely." The fellow appeared to be absorbed in his manicure, but Lisa suspected he was alert for any sudden movements on her part.

She didn't want to struggle with this man. She wanted to stay safe so she could return to Ryder and try to make him understand that she hadn't left on purpose.

"My parents want to marry me off to Boris," she said. "So, why would he do a thing like this?"

"He'll be wearing a disguise," said Lothaire. "He thinks he can have the ransom *and* your dowry."

"What point is there in his wearing a disguise, since you already told me it's him?"

"You would have recognized his voice, anyway." The man examined his cuticles.

"How does he hope to get away with this?"

"I told you, he's an idiot." Lothaire glanced up with a twist of a smile. "He's not going to get away with it, but I am."

Now she was even more frightened. Boris had nothing to gain by her death, but what about this man? "I don't understand."

He must have noticed her reaction. "Don't worry. Do as I say and you're in no danger. Please, Miss Dé La Pena, have a seat." He indicated a bolted-down couch. "I can get you a drink or a snack, if you like."

"Later." Her throat felt dry, but Lisa wanted to hear the rest of this. However, she sank onto the couch obediently.

"The fact is, your suitor owes a great deal of money to some very impatient people."

"Anyone I know?"

"Not if you're wise," said Lothaire. "These very impatient people sent me to work for him. As his trusted assistant, I suggested that he marry a rich woman so he could pay them back. However, you had the good sense to reject him, and off you went to America."

"I think I'm following this so far," she said.

"Our next idea, once we learned your returning flight schedule, was to nab you in New York and drug you while a marriage was performed," Lothaire said. "Instead, there was an unfortunate accident."

Lisa's hand flew to the stitches on her head. "*You* did this?"

"Not intentionally." The man resheathed his knife. "It might still have worked until, to our astonishment you disappeared from the hospital. You are a very elusive woman, Miss De La Pena."

"Not elusive enough, it seems."

"Since you were suffering from amnesia and likely to remain out of sight for a while, we decided to pretend that you had been kidnapped and demand a ransom. Tomorrow we will produce you, and your parents will pay us $1.5 million."

"You're going to take it and dump Boris," Lisa said.

"So you see," Lothaire continued as calmly as if discussing a luncheon menu, "I have no reason to harm you as long as you cooperate. Furthermore, when this business is over, you should have no trouble convincing your parents to break the engagement."

She almost laughed at the irony. "You've got this all worked out."

"So we hope."

Lisa thought about the $1.5 million her parents

would be turning over to Lothaire. As far as she was concerned, that money could come from her dowry.

The only man she wanted to marry was Ryder. She knew he wouldn't take a penny for her—if he would take her at all.

"The only thing you have to do," Lothaire said as he took two cans of soda from a small refrigerator, "is keep Boris in the dark about this entire conversation."

"I think I can manage that," said Lisa.

WITH THE LITTLE FRENCH he could muster, Ryder checked his luggage at the train station. If he'd come on a wild-goose chase, he reflected as he emerged into a light rain, he'd at least come to the right country to get some good pâté out of it.

Before him, the town bustled with Monday-morning activity. Motor scooters and bicycles wove between produce trucks, and fresh-baked bread perfumed the air. Red and yellow umbrellas bloomed along the sidewalks.

There was no sign of a car-rental place, so Ryder surveyed the vicinity for a taxi. He didn't see one.

"*Pardon,*" he said to a scarf-wrapped woman with a basket over her arm. "*Où se trouve le château?*"

"*Là,*" she said. There. And pointed.

Atop a hill in the distance stood a white palace, turreted and tower studded. Sleeping Beauty's Castle hadn't been far off the mark, Ryder realized. "*Est-ce qu'il y a un taxi?*"

"*Un taxi, ici?*" The woman whooped as if he'd said something hilarious. "*Vous avez deux pieds, monsieur! Voilà votre taxi!*"

He didn't need a translator for that one. You have two feet, monsieur. They are your taxi!

"Merci." Ryder wished he could get more information from the woman, but he didn't know enough French. Besides, what would he ask? He doubted the De La Penas had made a public announcement of where they intended to pay off their daughter's kidnapper.

Stepping across a mud puddle, Ryder made his way along a narrow sidewalk between dark-timbered buildings. A half hour later he left the town and started along a road that led toward the château through a vineyard.

The way ran upward, and a current of mud flowed past. The rain thickened, blurring his vision and, as he trudged, two days' worth of exhaustion hit Ryder in the face like a gust of water-laced wind.

Fierce resolve had powered him this far, but now he recognized that he had no particular plan, let alone any real information about what lay ahead. Perhaps the De La Penas had arranged some other site entirely, he thought morosely. Or had already made the payment.

What good would it do Lisa if he arrived at her doorstep like a sodden stray dog? He'd passed an inn in the village where he could clean up and rest for a few hours until the rain eased. It was time to yield to common sense.

As he wavered, a faint buzz caught Ryder's attention. He could see nothing through the gray clouds, and then the noise came again, louder and closer.

Through the clouds broke a low-flying helicopter, aiming toward a not-far-distant field.

Ryder broke into a lope.

Chapter Fifteen

Lisa wished Boris would stop humming. For one thing he was off-key. For another, it·was unseemly for him to be so cheerful about betraying his fiancée and her family.

And why on earth had he chosen a Richard Nixon mask with which to disguise himself? Its solemnity made the humming even more inappropriate.

The helicopter bumped on an air current, sending her stomach into flip-flops. She'd never ridden in a chopper before, and she certainly wouldn't have chosen to make her maiden voyage in a rainstorm.

The rest of the flight from America had passed smoothly. She and Lothaire had played cards for a while, but he couldn't resist cheating. Once she started cheating back, however, they got along fine.

Things had changed as soon as they'd landed at a private airport outside Paris and met up with Boris. She'd felt anxious, exhausted and just plain cranky. Her head wound hurt, and she itched to wash her hair.

Mostly she couldn't stand being near Boris, who had practically breathed down her neck all night and who sat beside her now. Even through that ridiculous mask, she could feel his smugness. It was enough to make her want to punch him in the nose.

She stared down at the clouds and the patches of gray countryside. She could imagine the musky scent of grapes and the spicy richness of leaves crushed beneath the downpour. California sunshine belonged to another universe.

Where was Ryder? Had he read her scribblings about getting pregnant? What was he thinking?

Lisa pictured him as she'd first seen him, waiting his turn on the ski slope. Through the binoculars, she'd been impressed by his well-shaped body and powerful stance.

She remembered him relaxed in bed, after his passion had been spent, and the way they'd nestled together. The way he'd gazed at her at the chalet, a bit puzzled but mellow. Beginning to care, to let himself go.

Later, at his apartment, she'd witnessed something deeper. Love? So she had begun to hope.

She might never see that look on his face again.

Lisa clamped her lips together as drops pelted the skin of the helicopter. The humid air made her feel clammy, and the sensation got worse every time Boris shifted in his seat and poked his legs against hers.

"Would you cut that out?" she growled.

"Do not forget, you are my preeezoner," he whined over the engine noise, in a high, fake voice.

In front of them, beside the pilot, Lothaire's shapely ears pricked up. Lisa guessed he was almost as eager to conclude this business as she was.

They arced over a windbreak of trees. Beyond it she spotted a four-wheel-drive vehicle with four people visible inside. The chopper veered past them and circled the field.

"Who are those other people?" screeched Boris in his falsetto. "There should be only your parents!"

Their swooping made Lisa's lunch spring to unpleasant life, but she tried to ignore it. "They brought the butler, Sebastien, and my maid, Mireille. It looks like they've got blankets."

"A wise precaution," observed Lothaire. "In case she gets chilled or goes into shock."

"They could be hiding weapons," squeaked Boris.

Lisa's father knew how to shoot a pistol, since his business took him to unsettled parts of the world. But she doubted he would use one here. "My father would never risk my life. Or that you might shoot back and hit my mother."

"After all," Lothaire pointed out, "it's only a million and a half dollars. To Schuyler De La Pena, that's chicken feed."

Compared to the well-being of his family, Lisa thought.

"We have to make sure the bills are real," Boris continued. "Lothaire, when you pick up the suitcase, take the time to open it."

"Of course I will make a quick inspection," he said.

"Not too quick!"

"It is a tense situation," said Lothaire. "We do not want to linger."

"We will linger as long as *I* see fit!" Boris flared. "Don't forget who is the brains of this operation."

As Lothaire turned away, Lisa caught the quirk of his mouth and wondered if he were thinking the same thing she was.

Boris is an idiot. But he's an idiot who has created a lot of trouble.

RYDER EDGED along the row of trees, keeping beneath the dripline so as not to be seen from the helicopter.

Between the roar of the engine and the sweep of the rain, he didn't have to worry about anyone hearing the occasional cracked twig. Still, he stopped some distance from the vehicle that he assumed belonged to the De La Penas.

As the chopper lowered toward earth, two people got out of the vehicle's front seat. They were followed by two deferential figures from the back, evidently servants.

The tall, striking woman opening a black umbrella must be Lisa's mother, Ryder thought. He could see a resemblance, although she had a remote air that her daughter lacked.

Nearby, hands fisted, a short, intense figure that must be Schuyler De La Pena paced through the downpour. With his snub nose and bulldog frame, he looked more like a street fighter than an aristocrat.

Ryder watched the military-style chopper make several tours of the field, then aim for a spot near the center. His heart wedged in his throat as he waited to see if Lisa were on board.

What if something went wrong? He hadn't brought a gun. At best, he might be able to create a distraction, but could anyone take advantage of it?

The copter set down, its rotors flattening the tall grass. Any identifying marks had been removed from its exterior, Ryder noted.

He had to hand it to Boris Grissofsky. The man had done a masterful job, kidnapping a woman in

California and bringing her all this distance, across borders and through changes of aircraft, without drawing suspicion.

Either he'd had a great deal of time to prepare—unlikely, under the circumstances—or he had underworld connections. Not a pleasant prospect.

Although it went against his instincts, Ryder knew his best bet was simply to wait this out. If no one played any tricks, the ransom should be handed over and Lisa safely restored to her family.

He tried not to think about how frightened she must be. Or whether she might have been injured in the abduction.

A door opened in the side of the chopper. Through tree branches and sheets of water, Ryder made out a blurry figure jumping down, swathed in a trench coat and broad-brimmed hat.

Too big to be Lisa, and moving with masculine ease. What he could see of the man's face appeared young and smooth.

Could this be Boris? Ryder detected no sign of surprise from the De La Penas, so perhaps not.

The man crossed to them and, Ryder gathered, was demanding the ransom. Schuyler shook his head and gestured at the craft.

Smart man. Get your daughter before you make the payoff.

As if on cue, a slender figure appeared in the doorway. Lisa!

Ryder started forward, then caught himself. Waiting beside a rain-blackened tree trunk, he watched her jump to the ground and wince at the impact.

Dark hair straggled around her face, and even in the filtered light she looked pale. But she was clearly moving under her own steam as she walked toward her parents.

Mrs. De La Pena took a step forward, but paused when her husband shouted, ''Valeria! Stay clear of the helicopter!''

Lisa broke into a run, stumbling, until she reached her mother's arms. At the same time, Schuyler retrieved a briefcase from the vehicle.

Ryder released a long breath. Things appeared to be going smoothly. Just let the abductor take the ransom and leave.

His attention snapped to the helicopter doorway. Who was that bulky man standing there? The one wearing a Richard Nixon mask?

Lisa hadn't noticed him yet. But Schuyler De La Pena had. He stood holding the briefcase, not releasing it to the man in the trench coat.

Ryder couldn't imagine why anyone would want to complicate a hostage release that was going so smoothly. Dismayed, he watched as the masked figure dropped to the ground, stumped across the field and grabbed the briefcase.

Schuyler held on for a moment, and it looked as if there might be a tug-of-war. Then Lisa's father let go.

The bulky man plopped the case to the ground, knelt and flipped the catches. Ryder tensed, half expecting to hear an explosion or see paint shoot out.

The man lifted out a bundled stack of bills and leafed through it. He replaced it and took out another pile, then another.

What was this clown going to do, count the entire ransom? His accomplice shouted something incomprehensible to Ryder, but it didn't take a linguist to understand the man was hurrying him.

At last the newcomer closed the suitcase and gave a satisfied nod. With a gesture toward his companion, he turned back toward the copter.

Then he swung around again, a revolver in his hand.

Shocked expressions flashed across the faces of everyone present. The other kidnapper took a step backward.

"I heard you on the phone last night, Lothaire," the large man sneered in the heavily accented English of Mr. Smith, alias Grissofsky, Ryder assumed. "I heard what you and the pilot are planning. You will never make a fool out of me!" He swung the gun toward Schuyler De La Pena. "I need your car, and I will be taking your daughter with me for insurance."

"No!" cried Valeria.

"Yes," said the man in the mask.

Ryder couldn't let him take Lisa again. He was too unstable and, with the ransom in hand, no longer had a strong motive for releasing her unharmed.

Grissofsky possessed a gun and control of the situation. The only thing going for Ryder was the element of surprise, so he kept to cover as he scooted quietly toward the far side of the vehicle.

"I'll take that briefcase, Boris." From within his jacket, the accomplice pulled an automatic pistol.

"Boris?" Mrs. De La Pena's voice broke on the second syllable. "Boris Grissofsky?"

"One and the same," said his companion smoothly. "Let's cut our losses, shall we, Boris? Bring the ransom and we'll both get out of here alive."

A snarl emanated from behind the mask, and then

its wearer ripped it off. The square, jowly face beneath didn't look all that different from the caricature of Nixon.

"You'll pay for this, you traitor," he barked.

The other man shrugged. "I think not. You're the one who owes money, and I'm here to collect it."

Just let Lisa go, Ryder ordered the kidnappers silently. *Get in the helicopter and fight over the ransom somewhere else.*

"You work for the Russians?" demanded Grissofsky.

"Yes. So you might as well hand it over, because sooner or later they'll find you."

"I didn't go through all this to come up empty-handed!"

Crouching, Ryder sprang from the shelter of the trees. Rain matted his hair and dripped from his forehead as he raced toward the four-wheel-drive.

No one noticed him. They were all riveted on the scene playing itself out in their midst.

Without warning, Boris dodged toward Valeria, seized Lisa and pulled her in front of him. It was a clumsy maneuver, since he had the briefcase tucked under one arm and the revolver in his hand, but with the barrel wavering near her ear, Lisa was in no position to fight.

"Well, Lothaire?" challenged Boris. "Are you willing to shoot the girl to get me?"

The automatic pointed straight at Lisa. Ryder's muscles tightened and his hands itched to grab a weapon, but there was nothing nearby, not even a rock.

The barrel swung away. "It's not my job to shoot innocent women," said Lothaire.

"Good." Keeping Lisa in front of him, Boris angled toward the four-wheel drive. "Stay back and nobody gets hurt."

"Take the car but leave my daughter!" cried Schuyler.

"Do you take me for a fool?"

"Please! Just let her go!"

"Not until it suits me."

In that moment, Lisa's gaze met Ryder's through the open vehicle. Her eyes widened in shock.

He mimed a quick ducking motion. If only she would trust him enough to obey without question!

His meaning took a second to register. Then, without hesitation, Lisa ducked.

Ryder plunged across the seat, heedless of the steering wheel's bruising impact on his thigh and the fact that he'd left one shoe stuck in the mud. Propelling himself over Lisa's head, he smashed into Boris and sent them both thudding to earth.

Boris dropped the briefcase and Lisa, but he still had the revolver. As Ryder struggled to regain his balance, the other man wiggled like a greased pig until he got his arm clear to take aim.

"No!" Lisa kicked at his wrist. "I won't let you!"

With a deafening blast, the gun went off. A bullet whistled so close that Ryder could feel the powder burn, and his ears rang like carillons.

The explosion knocked Boris flat. At the same time, it triggered Schuyler De La Pena into a frenzy of action. Shouldering Ryder aside, he flung himself on top of the fallen Boris and began pounding him with his fists, screaming, "I'll kill you!"

Beneath the onslaught, Boris's face crumpled like a papier-mâché mask left out in a storm. On the grass,

Valeria hurried to pick up both the gun and the briefcase before the accomplice could reach them.

Holding them defiantly, she glared at Lothaire. After a moment's consideration, he holstered his automatic and strode away.

A fresh burst of rain obscured Ryder's vision where he sat, his head throbbing. He could see only smeary shapes, including one breaking into a lope toward the helicopter.

"Are you all right?" Frantic hands pulled at his jacket. "He didn't hit you, did he?"

Lisa. She smelled wonderful, kneeling in the rain, her hair trailing across Ryder's chest as she examined him feverishly. Essence of wildflower mingled with fear and passion made a heady perfume.

He couldn't resist digging his fingers into that hair. Turning her face toward his, he caught a startled glint of green eyes, and then he kissed her.

She tasted even better than she smelled. Fiercely alive, hungry, and all his.

"I've never been better," he said when he came up for air. "How about you?"

Her arms tightened around him. "I can't believe you're here."

"Help!" wheezed Boris a few feet away. "He's killing me!"

With an exclamation of disgust, Schuyler quit pounding him. "Sebastien! *Ici!*"

The butler approached, carrying a rope. He and his employer rolled the whimpering captive and bound his hands behind his back.

"Oh, Ryder!" Lisa pressed her cheek to his chest. "You saved my life!"

"Saved your life?" roared her father. "This maniac nearly got you shot! Ryder? Ryder Kelly? Sebastien, tie him also!''

Ryder stared at Lisa's father in disbelief. Was it possible Schuyler De La Pena had misunderstood the situation, or did he simply resent seeing his daughter in the arms of a man who lacked the proper pedigree?

''Monsieur?'' said the puzzled butler, who was trying to drag Boris upright.

''Tie him?'' Lisa came up for air. ''You're crazy, Papa. He came here to rescue me, and this is how you thank him?''

''He came here because he wants a piece of your fortune.'' With a grimace her father indicated the briefcase. ''Why don't you give him the money and tell him to leave? I'll bet he'll take it, and gladly.''

The man was hopeless. ''Lisa,'' Ryder said, ''we should get out of the rain before you catch pneumonia. There's an inn at the village where we can scrape this mud off.''

''Don't go.'' Her mother spoke with a soft, Spanish-accented voice. ''I saw how you risked your life, Mr. Kelly. We owe you a great debt.''

The butler stuffed Boris into the back seat of the vehicle. He showed no interest in coming after Ryder.

''A debt?'' Schuyler said. ''For all we know, he was involved in this mess from the beginning. Maybe he's in league with that other kidnapper, the double-crosser. What do you think, Boris?''

Even now, Ryder thought in amazement, Lisa's father would seek advice from a proven criminal, as long as he had noble blood.

''In league? Who knows?'' snarled Boris. ''In any case I assume she's already paid him to make her pregnant.''

Schuyler made a choking noise. Valeria gasped.

"Why are you both so shocked?" Lisa cried. "That's why I ran off, to give you people the heir you wanted so much. But I certainly didn't pay Ryder!"

"You intended to have a baby with a stranger?" said her mother. "Annalisa, how could you?"

"There was no need to do such a foolish thing," said her father. "We had everything arranged."

"For me to marry this lowlife because he's related to the Hohnersteins?" Lisa cried. "Do you know he owes money to gangsters and that his business is a wreck?"

"It sounds to me," said her father firmly, "as if you need a long rest, Lisa."

"No," she said. "What I need is to stop acting like a teenager and start acting like an adult."

"You will do as I say!"

"She'll do as she pleases." Ryder would have liked to stand up, but Lisa was sitting on his lap. "Believe me, this lady doesn't take orders from anybody."

"You're on French soil now, *monsieur.*" Schuyler removed a cellular phone from his pocket, sheltering it with his body against the rain. "The police can deal with you."

"Monsieur, vous êtes un monstre!" The cry came from the maid, who until this point had huddled silently behind the others. Why was she calling her employer a monster? Ryder wondered, not that he wouldn't gladly second the motion.

"Mireille?" said Lisa. "What do you mean?"

"I gave that other man information. That Lothaire." The woman stepped forward tearfully. "I did not do it for money. I thought I was helping to promote a romance of true love for *mademoiselle*. I thought that young man was enamored of her. I wished to help her escape because you treated her like a prisoner!''

''Prisoner?'' asked Valeria.

''You're fired!'' said Schuyler.

''I quit!'' said the maid.

''I think we should get out of the rain,'' said Ryder.

Lisa sneezed. That settled it.

Chapter Sixteen

Lisa hated letting go of Ryder. She didn't feel cold until the air rushed between them, and then nothing could warm her, not even the blankets that her mother and Sebastien kept piling on her as they jounced back to the château in the vehicle.

It infuriated Lisa that her father insisted on being so irrational. At least he calmed down enough so that, by the time the police came to take Boris, he was no longer suggesting that Ryder should be arrested. He also rehired Mireille, who apologized profusely for her role in the abduction.

But Lisa could tell that her father expected her to go back to being his little girl, the one who'd accepted being shut away in the château. The one who'd been afraid to confront her parents for fear of losing them.

She scarcely knew that girl. Lisa's memories had returned, but they might have belonged to a different person.

What mattered now was Ryder. That he hadn't turned away when he learned the truth about why she'd sought him out.

Still, she knew better than to read too much into his actions. An honorable man like him might have felt guilty for leaving her alone at the store on Saturday. Or perhaps obligation upon learning that she might be carrying his child.

Now that he'd made sure she was safe and well taken care of, his duty had ended. He owed her nothing.

Nothing that he did not want to give freely.

As soon as she dried off and changed clothes, Lisa went in search of him.

Her parents had put Ryder in the Marie Antoinette chamber. It was rumored that the ill-fated queen had slept there once, and, as Lisa recalled, the ornate furnishings and sumptuous bed coverings reflected that long-ago era.

She knocked twice. Hearing no answer, she went in, anyway.

She'd forgotten the immensity of the room, like a gymnasium, and the rococo excesses of wallpaper, draperies, moldings, china knickknacks and carved furniture that stuffed the place. How must it look to a man who never bothered to hang a picture on a wall?

Seeing no sign of him, she started toward the inner door that led to the bath chamber. It opened as she approached.

In a blast of steam Ryder emerged with a towel wrapped around his midsection. Wet, freshly combed hair clung to his well-shaped head. Along his bare torso, muscles rippled, and with a flare of longing Lisa remembered how it felt to run her hands over his chest.

He stopped short, nearly on top of her. "Lisa! I didn't realize you were here."

She could read nothing in his face. Several opening

lines ran through her mind, but she rejected them all and waited until Ryder spoke again.

"One of the servants was supposed to pick up my suitcase at the train station. I wonder if he's done it." He walked to a freestanding mahogany wardrobe and opened it to reveal several suits and shirts, which he must have thrown in his bag haphazardly before his flight, perfectly pressed and hanging in place. "Good heavens! What efficiency."

"Say something." Lisa lowered herself onto the edge of the bed. "Please."

He turned, nearly dropped the towel and yanked it back into place. "I was under the impression I *was* saying something."

"Don't talk about your clothes. Tell me why you came."

Ryder fumbled to get a drawer open, took out some underwear and put it on under the towel. "You were in trouble," he said, tossing the towel aside.

"Aren't you angry? That I used you to try to get pregnant?" She desperately needed some sign of his mood.

"Are you? Pregnant?"

"I don't know. It hasn't been long enough to tell."

The scar on his temple flashed as he removed a white shirt from the wardrobe and slipped it on. His dark eyes had barely flicked at her, Lisa realized, and now they were focused a thousand light-years away.

Was he angry? Bored? She'd never been good at forcing issues, but heaven knew when they would have another chance to talk. "First of all, I'm sorry."

"How sorry?" He buttoned his cuffs.

"Acutely," she said.

This time he regarded her directly. "What's second?"

"Excuse me?"

"You said, 'First of all.' What comes next?"

"Can I hit you with something?" she asked. "Tell me where you *don't* hurt, and I'll hit you there."

A smile animated his face. "I don't hurt anywhere. Come pummel me wherever you please."

Lisa didn't know what to make of this sudden change in mood. "I don't want to hit you. I just want your attention."

Ryder reached into another drawer and extracted a newspaper. Holding it, he came and sat beside her. "Take a look at this."

Confused, Lisa studied the paper. It was the real estate section of the *Los Angeles Times*. "Is there a hidden message? Some kind of code?"

He opened it to a double-page spread showing new homes. "I wondered if you prefer the Mediterranean style or the Tudor. Frankly, I think Tudor is pretentious in Southern California, but don't let that influence you."

The truth dawned. "You're asking me to pick a house?"

"With the bonus I earned Saturday, while you were so inconveniently getting yourself abducted, I can afford the down payment," Ryder said. "That is, if you can tear yourself away from all this—" his gesture encompassed a gilded mantel clock and a group of china shepherdesses "—froufrou."

Lisa began to laugh. "I *hate* all this froufrou! Mediterranean sounds perfect!"

Muscular arms gathered her close. She burrowed

into him, inhaling his freshly showered manliness and relishing the whisper of his lips against her ear.

"Je t'aime," said Ryder.

"Te amo."

"Ich liebe dich. Did I say that right?"

"Perfectly."

"I love you." Ryder brushed a wisp of hair from her cheek. "When I saw Boris drag you toward the vehicle... I've been frightened, plenty of times. But I've always known that I would either live or I'd die, and if I lived, no matter how badly injured, I could go on. But not if I let something happen to you, Lisa. I couldn't live with that."

"What about children?" she asked. "You didn't want them."

"That was in the abstract," he murmured. "It's like abstract art. It doesn't necessarily portray reality."

Lisa couldn't believe it. "You won't feel trapped or cheated? We never have to worry about being poor, you know."

"Is that a reference to the fabled dowry?"

"Sort of." She held her breath, wondering if she'd offended him.

"Keep it in trust for our kids' education," he said. "I can support my own family."

"Kids, plural?"

"We wouldn't want them to get lonely." He grinned. "Do you suppose your parents would mind if we didn't go downstairs for a few hours?"

"They might mind, but *I* wouldn't."

IT WAS DINNERTIME before they made their way down the grand staircase, through immense tapestried spaces and into a dining room the size of Grand Central Station.

Ryder could hardly believe this place belonged to a single family. What did the De La Penas plan to do, hold in-line skating competitions indoors?

The wonderful release of lovemaking, followed by a much-needed hour of sleep, had refreshed him. He had taken yet another shower and put on his best suit, which was almost identical to his worst suit.

One glance at Schuyler and Valeria, standing beside a sideboard drinking wine from crystal glasses, and Ryder knew he'd fallen short of their standards yet again. Lisa's father wore a black-and-white tuxedo; her mother, a high-necked amber gown that swept the floor.

Lisa herself returned from her room in a scoop-necked blue dress with flowing sleeves cuffed at the wrist. She looked, he thought, like a princess in a fairy tale.

They said little as they took their seats and servants brought the first course. Ryder found himself presented with a plateful of garlicky escargots.

"You don't have to eat them," murmured Lisa, seated opposite him. They were halfway down the immense table from her parents.

"Is something wrong with the food?" asked her father icily. "Don't tell me you're squeamish about snails."

Ryder immediately suspected him of ordering these on purpose. "Do you raise them on the estate?"

"Hardly," said Valeria.

"I'm sure we'll have lots of them in our garden," Ryder said. "But don't worry, Lisa. I'll stock up on snail bait."

She nearly choked, trying to stifle a laugh. Schuyler sputtered in annoyance.

"Your garden?" said Valeria.

A poignant silence hung over the table until Lisa explained, "We're getting married."

As he waited for his future in-laws' response, Ryder noticed a cupid winking at him from the mural on the dining room wall. Oddly, he felt neither defensive nor boastful, but completely at peace.

Somewhere between knocking Boris-who-is-distantly-related-to-the-Hohnersteins into the mud and seducing Lisa in Marie Antoinette's bed, Ryder had ceased to resent their snobbery.

It simply no longer mattered. To him the attitudes of the rich had become an affectation, like getting one's nose pierced or claiming to have read books when you'd only seen the movie. If it made the perpetrators happy, why should he care?

He felt Schuyler De La Pena's assessing gaze and awaited a torrent of objections. Instead the man said, "I don't suppose you have any experience in running a business, do you, Mr. Kelly?"

"Only my detective agency."

"I'm considering opening a branch in America," Schuyler went on coolly. "I would prefer to keep the management in the family."

"You're offering me a job?" said Ryder.

"Naturally, we would have to work out the details."

"I don't even know what kind of business you're in," Ryder said. "But it doesn't sound like my cup of tea. Thanks, anyway."

"Even in the United States, it's hard for people to find parts for any product that isn't the latest model."

The man patted his mouth lightly with his cloth napkin. "I think we could do well there."

"You'll do even better if you have a service department," Lisa said. "And you'll need to plan a big splashy opening with a major advertising campaign. Make it more chic to repair old stuff than to buy new."

"Surely you don't expect me to offer *you* the presidency! You're not hard-headed enough for this kind of thing," said her father.

"I don't want to work twenty hours a day, either, especially since I plan on having children," she said. "I was just offering a little helpful advice."

"You wouldn't want to head up our American branch?" her father asked in disbelief.

"I might consider a consulting position," said Lisa. "If I could work part-time."

Ryder fought back a grin. As far as he was concerned, his wife could pursue any career she wanted, but now that he'd warmed to the idea of children, he relished the prospect of both parents spending lots of time with them.

Valeria De La Pena broke the silence. "I think our daughter has done very well for herself. You wanted grit, Schuyler. Here it is, in both of them."

"Grit?" Ryder arched an eyebrow.

"My father wants feisty grandchildren," Lisa explained. "That's how this whole...situation got started."

"We shouldn't have tried to push you into a marriage," her mother admitted. "But you seemed to be drifting through life."

"I was afraid of losing your love if I stood up to

you,'' their daughter admitted. ''You never approved of anything I did on my own.''

''You thought we would stop loving you?'' Her father set down his fork. ''Lisa, you mean more to us than anything in the world.''

''More than all the money,'' said Valeria.

''More than my own life,'' said Schuyler.

Lisa's eyes glistened. Her lips twitched, and then she pushed back her chair and raced to hug her parents with such a rush of emotion that, had Ryder not held on to the tablecloth, she would have taken it and half the dishes with her.

Unwillingly he found his thoughts yanked to his own mother. As a young man, he'd blamed her for her poor choice in husbands, but she'd done her best to support him and his sisters.

According to last year's Christmas cards from his sisters, Mom was single again and living near San Francisco. It was time, he decided, to get back in touch with her. Long past time.

''Well, son?'' demanded Schuyler, and Ryder realized the man was standing. ''Aren't you going to shake my hand?''

''It would be my pleasure, sir.'' He made his way to the head of the table and shook hands firmly. Then he accepted a warm hug from Valeria.

''It's been hard for me to accept that my trust in Boris was misplaced,'' admitted Lisa's father. ''But on reflection, Mr. Kelly, I have to concede that you're exactly the sort of son-in-law I sought. Independent, tough-minded and devoted to your wife.''

''A lot like you, dear,'' murmured Valeria, slipping one arm through her husband's.

''Did I tell you how he saved a little girl on the

ski slope the first time I saw him?'' asked Lisa. ''And how he rescued me at the beach?''

''All that in a little over a week?'' said her mother.

''Ryder does this kind of thing all the time!'' chirped Lisa.

''Not exactly.'' He knew his cheeks must be reddening. Ryder had never had anyone boast about him this way. He felt as if he were listening to someone else's exploits.

''I myself witnessed your conduct today,'' Schuyler conceded as they took their places again at the table. ''It was difficult for me to admit, but you deserve the credit for foiling Boris's plans. I'm sorry I let my pride get in the way.''

''Do tell us about the other adventures!'' said Valeria, entranced.

Lisa launched into the tale of the little girl on the ski run. As the servants brought the rest of the meal, Ryder noticed that they lingered in the background, listening in fascination.

The person enjoying it most was Lisa herself. Watching as her eyes sparkled and her skin glowed, Ryder felt his chest swell with a warm and delirious sensation that had to be love.

Come to think of it, she'd done plenty of daring deeds herself, including marching out of a hospital in New York despite her amnesia and finding Ginger at the beach.

He could scarcely wait until she concluded the tales about him, so he could tell his wonderful stories about her.

Even Schuyler De La Pena was going to be impressed.

"THE HAT was definitely a wise choice," said Nicola. "So much more stylish than a veil."

"And *much* better than a gag and a blindfold, eh?" said Maureen ruefully.

"I don't know," sighed Buffy. "I think a headband of flowers would look pretty."

"She's not getting married on the beach!" reproved Starr. "This is a palace! She can't just stick a few daisies in her hair."

Lisa gazed in the mirror at the friends grouped around her. What an unlikely bunch they were, too!

Nicola wore her golden gown elegantly and her chestnut hair—the gray recently expunged—in a sophisticated French twist. She'd been enjoying the prenuptial festivities, the more so because her role as maid of honor thrust her once more into the center of society.

A simpler dress in a quieter shade suited Maureen's open looks and wedge-cut red hair. She'd been more subdued than usual since breaking up with her perfidious boyfriend, but Lisa had no doubt she would bounce back quickly.

As for Starr and Buffy, being treated to their first trip to France and welcomed into a château had thrilled the girls beyond measure. Their rose pink dresses had been artfully conceived by the couturier as both suitable to their ages and a complement to the other gowns.

Taken as a group, the four reminded Lisa of a bouquet of flowers in mingled golds and pinks, with a white rose at the center.

She could hardly believe this radiant bride was her. Although Lisa had always assumed that someday she would marry, she'd envisioned the event as simply a necessary prelude to taking her place in the role her parents cut out for her.

The woman gazing back at her in the oval glass had a few familiar characteristics: the aristocratic De La Pena jawline, for instance, and familiar tendrils of black hair curling from beneath the silk hat. But in those green eyes burned new confidence and determination and love.

"I can't believe this is me," she admitted. "I can't believe I found Ryder, out of all the men in the world."

"It's amazing what you can turn up on the Internet, eh?" joked Maureen.

"I suppose we have to thank Win for that," Lisa admitted.

"Even if he was a rat," said her friend.

"The world is full of rats," sighed Nicola. To Starr and Buffy, she added, "You must be very careful, girls. Before you marry a man, investigate him thoroughly. If you can, interview his ex-girlfriends."

"Good idea," said Buffy.

"Make sure he wouldn't sell you out for a few bucks," added Maureen. "Character is everything."

"I've never even gone out on a date," said Starr. "I don't think I need to worry about this yet."

"Well, I knew what *I* was getting," said Lisa. "Ryder came with recommendations."

"He's cool," said Buffy.

"Definitely," affirmed Starr.

"Where did you find these two little charmers?" asked Nicola. "I must take them under my wing. Would you girls like to visit me in Rome?"

"Yes!" they said.

"Can we try on your clothes?" asked Starr.

"All of them!" agreed Nicola.

As the others moved away, Lisa applied a final layer of lipstick. She bent toward the mirror and tried to ignore a sudden churning in her stomach.

She was *not* going to be sick. At four months along, she ought to be past that phase of her pregnancy, anyway.

The burning sensation subsided. Relieved, she studied herself again in the mirror and was grateful that the subtle pleats at the waistline hid her slight roundness.

Only her parents and Ryder knew about the baby. They had decided it would be discreet to wait another month, by which time her state would become obvious, to make the announcement.

A knock at the door drew Maureen's attention. She opened it to admit Schuyler.

"Are you lovely ladies ready?" he asked. "Everyone's waiting."

Lisa's father had been basking in the festivities all week, genially playing host to business acquaintances, his wife's friends and family, Parisian society and even Ryder's surprised and quite delightful sisters and mother.

The château had, for the first time since they'd bought it, been packed to the rafters with company. In her element, Valeria commanded an army of caterers, valets, seamstresses, florists and maids to keep the household running smoothly.

After all this fuss, Lisa was fervently looking forward to settling in their newly purchased home on a quiet cul-de-sac. Escrow had closed last month, and, Ryder had assured her when he returned a few days ago, most of their furniture was in place.

She couldn't wait to be alone with him. The man she loved. Her husband.

Her one concern these past weeks had been that Ryder's miraculous transformation would prove to be temporary. How could he show such forbearance in the face of so much wealth and pomp? Above all, could he really commit himself to a wife and children, when he had spent so much of his life battling for independence?

As she stood to take her father's arm, Lisa hoped her uncertainty didn't show. To everyone else, the pageantry of the wedding had taken on a life of its own.

But she knew what mattered. If Ryder had asked it, she would gladly have eloped with him.

Please let him be as happy as I am.

"You look pale." Schuyler leaned close to his daughter's ear. "Not feeling sick, are we?"

"Just nervous," she said.

"Want to sit down?"

She shook her head. A delay wouldn't help. Until she descended the staircase and saw Ryder's face as he waited for her, she couldn't find out what she needed to know.

Schuyler shooed the bridesmaids ahead of them, out the door and down the hallway. Picking up her bouquet of roses and summer flowers, Lisa leaned gratefully on her father's arm.

As they reached the head of the curving staircase, she could hear people shifting and murmuring below. The grand entryway and the main salon, with its doors thrown open, had been filled with chairs. Hundreds of them: she'd lost count of the number of guests attending.

She could smell the flowers that filled every corner. She pictured the white-draped altar and the family's minister waiting at one end, prayer book in hand, and heard the organ play the opening notes of a lovely melody by French composer Charles Gounod.

Ahead of her, Nicola wafted down the staircase to the oohs and ahhs of the guests. Lisa was pleased to know that, after this event, her friend would be restored to her position in society—if she wanted it.

Then it was Maureen's turn, her naturally jaunty step defying her attempts at decorum. Next went Starr, surprisingly dignified, followed by the elated Buffy. Lisa distracted herself by thinking how much their parents, among the guests, must be enjoying this scene.

The music segued into Mendelssohn's wedding march. Beside Lisa, Schuyler vibrated with eagerness.

She could scarcely force herself to move forward. Electric tingles invaded her joints, and had it not been for her father's support, her knees might have buckled.

Will I see panic on your face, Ryder? Are you feeling trapped?

The curve of the stairs hid from her view the man waiting below. Lifting the unfamiliar weight of her satin skirt in one hand, Lisa picked her way slowly.

A gasp went up as the guests caught sight of her gown. Its silken simplicity had been engineered to highlight her long neck and straight shoulders, and Lisa supposed she and her father made a stylish tableau.

Flashbulbs flared from below, nearly blinding her. Schuyler muttered his disapproval, although she knew he would enjoy the photographs later. There was an official wedding photographer, and Valeria had yielded to pleas by the couturier to admit a camera-woman from *Vogue* as well.

Lisa just wanted this part to be over. She wished everyone would go away. She ached to see Ryder's expression.

They came around a curve, and her vision blurred. She could make out the black and white of his tuxedo, nothing more.

Fiercely she blinked away the sheen of moisture and fixed on his handsome face.

For a moment she could read nothing in the firm lines of his cheeks and forehead. Then a lopsided grin transformed his face.

He winked, just the flicker of an eyelid, but Lisa knew he was sharing a private joke. *Look at all these people in their fancy clothes. Wouldn't we rather be doing something that requires no clothes at all?*

Her first impulse was to giggle. Her second was to climb onto the railing and slide the rest of the way down into his arms.

Lisa did neither. Somehow she managed to descend the rest of the steps with dignity, hand her bouquet to Nicola and stand calmly in place while the minister asked her father to give his daughter in marriage.

Ryder took her arm. A shaft of sunshine penetrated the tall, narrow windows and bathed the two of them in a pool of warm light. The three of them, Lisa amended, instinctively touching one hand to her abdomen.

Long after the guests had gone and the flowers had faded, after the wedding gown had been folded in tissue, she and Ryder and the baby would share the magic of this moment.

Forever.

He's every woman's fantasy, but only one woman's dream come true.

Harlequin American Romance brings you THE ULTIMATE...in romance, as our most sumptuous series continues. Because a guy's wealth, looks and bod are nothing without that one special woman.

THE ULTIMATE...

...Catch

#760 *RICH, SINGLE & SEXY*
Mary Anne Wilson
January 1999

...Lover

#762 *A MAN FOR MEGAN*
Darlene Scalera
February 1999

Don't miss any of The Ultimate...series!

Available at your favorite retail outlet.

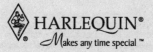

HARLEQUIN®
Makes any time special ™

If you enjoyed what you just read,
then we've got an offer you can't resist!

Take 2 bestselling love stories FREE!

Plus get a FREE surprise gift!

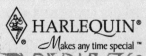

HARLEQUIN®

A M E R I C A N ❖ R O M A N C E®

COMING NEXT MONTH

Look us up on-line at: http://www.romance.net